C000092951

'Everyone has a number of alter-egos, however shadowy. I lived most of my life as though I were triplets. They shared an adequate but untutored brain, but as far as behaviour went it was touch and go between the three of them.

There was my father's daughter, swinging between romantic optimism and bewildered despair; a puritan, agonizingly shy but intolerant, rebellious but longing for acceptance, pouring it all out in writing which was little more than an elaboration of what had been poured in: passionate discontent, wild speculation.

Then there was the young woman my daughter Madelon adored, who knew the words of all the popular songs, danced like Ginger Rogers, behaved outrageously and was always beautiful . . .

The third and possibly most powerful was my mother's daughter: competent housewife, devoted mother, successful victim. From now on I shall lump these diverse personae together and call them, however inaccurately, myself.'

About Time Too

1940-1978

PENELOPE MORTIMER

W. A. Beaver
Woodborough
5th April 1999
Wilts.

PHŒNIX

A PHOENIX PAPERBACK

First published in Great Britain by
Weidenfeld & Nicolson in 1993
This paperback edition published in 1994
by Phoenix,
a division of Orion Books Ltd,
Orion House, 5 Upper St Martin's Lane,
London WC2H 9EA

Second impression 1994

Copyright © 1993 Penelope Mortimer

The right of Penelope Mortimer to be identified as the author
of this work has been asserted by her in accordance with the
Copyright, Designs and Patents Act 1988.

All rights reserved. No part of this publication may be
reproduced, stored in a retrieval system, or transmitted, in
any form or by any means, electronic, mechanical,
photocopying, recording or otherwise, without the prior
permission of the copyright owner.

A CIP catalogue record for this book is available from
the British Library.

ISBN: 1 85799 054 4

Printed and bound in Great Britain by
The Guernsey Press Co. Ltd,
Guernsey, C.I.

To fill a Gap
Insert the Thing that caused it —
Block it up
With Other — and 'twill yawn the more —
You cannot solder an Abyss
With Air.

Emily Dickinson

Scarcely anything in literature is worth a damn except
what is written between the lines.

Raymond Chandler to Bernice Baumgarten 13.2.49

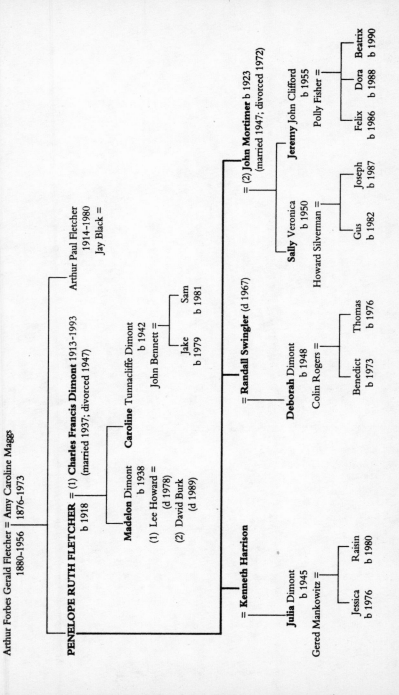

Illustrations appear between pages 84 and 85

The photographs have been selected from
the Author's collection and from the
Mark Gerson photo library.

For Madelon, Caroline, Julia, Deborah, Sally and Jeremy, because and in spite of.

Prologue

About Time, the first volume of my life, ended on my twenty-first birthday, a fortnight after the beginning of World War II. I was married to Charles Dimont, a journalist working for Reuters. In March 1938 he was sent to Vienna to cover the Anschluss; our daughter Madelon was born there that summer. We returned to England in September, shortly before the Munich agreement.

This sequel begins in 1940. We had been married for almost three years; Madelon was eighteen-months-old. Charles, unemployed since Reuters gave him the sack the previous winter, had decided to be a conscientious objector. We had left our flat in Shepherd's Bush, Madelon and I to live with my parents in Worcestershire, Charles to the Pacifist Service Unit's headquarters in Chelsea.

* * *

My husband was an intelligent and sensitive young man, brought up by a mother who was, or had become, a nonentity, and a teetotal clergyman father who claimed that he had found no reason to change his mind about anything since making it up at the age of twenty-one. In search of mystery their son had taken to drink and the doctrines of heathen religions. My father too was a clergyman, but a man with such an insatiable need for consolation that no faith could satisfy him. No longer finding any comfort in God, he gobbled samples of Communism, spiritualism, nudism, Nietzsche, free love, the Douglas Credit System, Krafft-Ebing, Freud, but was still ravenous. He went through terrible bouts of mourning for some satisfaction he couldn't remember or had never known and during these attacks the house would be chock-a-block with gloom, it was hard to find a breathing space. I inhaled his misery by the lungful, just as I did his tobacco smoke. My mother carried her own supply of wintry air. She and my father never shared a bedroom and I remember witnessing only one occasion when she didn't move away from his touch.

My father 'abused' me from the time I was eight until I was about seventeen; that is, his deprivation becoming unbearable, he tried to find some release in clumsy petting. It seldom went further than sloppy kisses and inexpert groping in my school knickers, but I hated it and for the next fifty years was under the sad misapprehension that I hated him. In fact, the shame and humiliation he so obviously suffered had a much greater effect on me than the so-called abuse. I suppose, in hindsight, it was a choice between pity and contempt. I was far too young for pity, and contempt was easy. Apart from this, and his doomed attempts to convert me to whatever faith he currently believed, my father appeared to contribute very little to my upbringing.

As my mother is one of the principal figures in this story, whether she is being mentioned or not, no more than a brief introduction is necessary. She was sixty-three when this book begins and looked a sprightly forty. Like many Victorian women brought up in Non-conformist homes, she was aggressively humble, blatantly self-effacing, passionately frigid. She lacked every maternal quality except faith in regular meals. She never hugged, kissed, consoled or explained. Carefully hidden under this stoic shell was a country girl of the 1880s with a hoard of manly brothers, a girl who whipped a pony trap through the Wiltshire lanes and doubled up laughing at the curate's devotion. Very occasionally she would show me this part of herself, the resigned expression crumpling into giggles, small hazel eyes brimming with glee. With my children she would be demonstrative, garrulous, sympathetic, even playful. Her intention, in which she succeeded, was to be the stable factor in their lives. I relied on her for everything except happiness.

I had a brother, Paul, who had been sent to boarding school at the age of four-and-a-half, just at the time I was born. Sixteen years later we struck up a brief friendship, but by 1939 we were again strangers. His implacable hatred of our father and mother lasted until his death in 1980. Our effect on each other and my feelings for him have yet to be discovered.

* * *

Everyone has a number of alter-egos, however shadowy. I lived most of my life as though I were triplets. They shared an adequate but untutored brain, but as far as behaviour went it was touch and go between the three of them.

There was my father's daughter, swinging between romantic optimism and bewildered despair; a puritan, agonizingly shy but intolerant, rebellious but longing for acceptance, pouring it all out in writing which was little more than an elaboration of what had been poured in: passionate discontent, wild speculation.

3

Then there was the young woman my daughter Madelon adored, who knew the words of all the popular songs, danced like Ginger Rogers, behaved outrageously and was always beautiful. Perhaps she had her origin in my mother's spark of flightiness; that's the nearest approach to frivolity I can find among the glum ranks of my ancestors. True, a few of them had 'gone to the bad' – at least one alcoholic, a couple of defrauders, a suicide. Imitation Ginger might have gone the same way if it hadn't been for her alter-ego's cumbersome conscience.

The third and possibly most powerful was my mother's daughter: competent housewife, devoted mother, successful victim. From now on I shall lump these diverse personae together and call them, however inaccurately, myself.

CHAPTER ONE

1

Willersey Rectory, Broadway, Worcs. — if I had been blindfolded and turned round on my axis a dozen times I should have known where I was the moment I went through the front door. My father chain-smoked Players Medium Cut cigarettes, varied by the occasional pipe. The impenetrable tobacco fog in his study seeped through the passages, solidified in the downstairs loo, drifted in great clouds into the dining room. Upstairs the air was clear, the smells mild and indistinguishable. My father never smoked in his bedroom, but began coughing the moment he closed the door, stopping only to sneeze six times, never more nor less. This nightly cacophony stopped abruptly when he got into bed. I remember timing it: six and a half minutes.

The temperature in the Rectory fluctuated between tropical and arctic. My father's study, on a lower level than the rest of the house, was a furnace, what with the smoke and his patent stove (I think it was called a 'Siesta') that stayed in all night, so long as the doors and damper were closed — forget either and there would be an appalling conflagration. He had installed one of these miracles in the dining room, but as it was a large room the heat petered out long before it reached the oak dresser with its Willow Pattern jugs and tureens, the oak gate-legged table and ladderback chairs — 'carvers' for my parents, unless my mother relinquished hers to the rare Archdeacon. In the winter I spent a great deal of time in this room, lying on the floor in front of the stove, grilling first one side, then the other, urgently writing in a hard-backed folio notebook.

When Charles managed to get to Willersey, always with a half-bottle of whisky in his pocket, he would sleep for forty-eight hours, make love to me and polite conversation to my parents, tell Madelon a story and shamble off in the direction of Honeybourne, not to be seen again for perhaps a couple of months. My mother was forbearing with him, though unable to understand my 'infatuation' — her term for sexual love. When my mother didn't understand something she tended to laugh, a melodious tinkle that was anything but amused. My father was grudgingly impressed by my father-in-law, the Chancellor of Salisbury Cathedral, but the thought of little Pegs having a legitimate sexual relationship with the Chancellor's son was intolerable, particularly when it went on in the next bedroom. He suffered dreadfully. I know that because of the incomprehensible letters he pushed under our bedroom door, written and rewritten in the cauldron of his study at five or maybe four o'clock in the morning.

Charles's objection to fighting, or violence of any kind, was loosely based on Aldous Huxley's *Ends and Means*. Rather to our surprise the Bristol Tribunal, headed by a Judge Wethered, respected the general idea and gave him unconditional exemption. It turned out that Charles and the Judge's son had been at Oxford together. The Judge then asked us out to lunch, in the

6

course of which he revealed that he was an avid ballroom dancer. Conscientious objectors must have been thin on the ground that afternoon, for I'm told that then and there he invited me to go dancing. Obviously I didn't accept. Fox-trotting with a Judge at a Bristol *thé-dansant* would surely be unforgettable.

2

There was a war on and although I thought myself a pacifist I was twenty-one-years-old, full of energy and dismayed at the prospect of being stuck in my parents' house for the duration. I decided to drive an ambulance, overlooking the fact that I couldn't drive. Since it didn't occur to me there were plenty of ambulances in nearby towns, I went back to London. There was no room on Charles's camp bed, no way that I could discover to learn how to drive and apparently no war. I remember nothing about it except the serene barrage balloons and the fine network of their tethers.

Apart from copious notes in green ink and many pencilled outbursts, I finished a novel in the autumn of 1939, unhappily titled *Time for Tenderness*. It was turned down with the usual sops of 'promise', 'shows distinction' etc. The writing hardly paused. What else was there to do? My father refused to teach me to drive, imagining his car dead in some ditch. My brother came for the occasional weekend, wearing rough khaki, taciturn. I know that I must have taken Madelon to stay with Charles's parents in Salisbury Close because I remember my mother-in-law fainting flat-out in her drawing room at the news of the Fall of France. I was no more gregarious then than I am now and knew none of the fresh-faced girls in hats and Brylcreemed boys who endured my father's sermons every Sunday. I didn't go to church. Except for Charles's rare weekend visits, writing, badly or better, was the only way of distinguishing between the days.

My mother suffered a great deal from this 'hobby' of mine. It meant that she had to look after my child as well as my father, myself, the shopping and cooking, the housework, the garden and the parish. It wasn't surprising that she was a little sharp with me at times. On the other hand she had long been convinced that I was morally handicapped, incapable of taking responsibility or managing the simplest domestic chore. This was a great grief to her but, as many mothers do, she blamed herself. Her self-inflicted punishment was to live my domestic life for me, as far as she was able.

If I stripped off one of Madelon's abundant cardigans it was immediately and silently replaced; if I washed her hair, my mother marched her straight back to the bathroom to give it another rinse. In the mornings, while I was sleeping soundly, she would fetch Madelon into her bed and feed her with quarters of peeled apple before washing and dressing her and taking her downstairs for a bowl of wholesome porridge. In the evenings, if the typewriter was pounding at the top of the house, my mother gave her a bath; then she would call up the stairs, asking if I wanted to say goodnight. I always did, though she insisted it wasn't necessary. Was I grateful for all this? No more than if Madelon had been my baby sister. Colluding, I reverted to being a sullen, difficult teenager, making plans for escape. We had no money.

My father's stipend was £650 a year and he was always in debt. My mother received a tiny annuity from one of her rich brothers but I suspect all of it was spent on feeding and clothing us. I knew escape was impossible. The only way of solving that problem was to ignore it.

'Where there's a will, there's a way,' my mother often said, though usually referring to learning algebra or how to sew on buttons; 'Grasp the nettle firmly.' I preferred this advice to her more usual 'It's no use kicking against the pricks.' When I was about seven-years-old I devised an elaborate demonstration of my omnipotence. First, with some difficulty, I would tie myself to the bed rail with my dressing gown cord. When it was fairly secure I would tell myself to walk across the room. Then I would deliberate, weighing up the pros and cons. Did I really *want* to walk across the room? The answer, curiously enough, was always the same: no, not really. This seemed to me satisfactory proof that everything in life was a matter of choice. The rule of cause and effect, which my mother called sowing and reaping, didn't apply to me. If I really wanted to do something, nothing was impossible. If I didn't, nothing could make me. In the intervening fourteen years I had doubted this belief only once, when I stood on the quay at Southampton watching the *Bremen* steaming out into the Channel with my first lover on board: the impossible was happening. Time softened the blow, even if it didn't wipe out the memory. With that one exception (and perhaps, after all, I had permitted it?) I still believed my will was irresistible.

Wootton, on the slope of Boar's Hill, is now a suburb of Oxford, but in 1941 it was a village. 'The Butts' stood, or rather leant, at right angles to the village street: whitewashed brick, tiled roof, two windows upstairs, a kind of french window let into the downstairs wall about a foot above ground level, a gable, a straggle of virginia creeper. The garden, flanked by a hedge on one side and a low wall on the other, consisted of grass, a plum tree, an ornamental stone mushroom and a derelict vegetable patch. I peered through the windows, walked round the garden, investigated the garage and then did whatever I had to do — telephone someone, I suppose — and took it without hesitation. The rent was one pound a week which Charles, when contacted, said he could afford. His father, to whom I piteously appealed, promised to contribute five pounds a week. I considered that problem solved.

My mother was incredulous. 'You mean you just *took* it? Without even going inside?' She was frantically worried about Madelon. The place was probably damp, insanitary. 'It's got plumbing, of course?' I didn't know. 'And electricity I *hope*?' I thought it might have electricity. The enormity of my irresponsibility overcame her. All she could manage was 'Oh Pegs ...' with an expiring sigh, as though she were giving up my ghost.

She provided furniture, curtains, coconut matting from her brother Will's hemp factory, saucepans, hot water bottles and a tea cosy. We moved sometime in March 1941. My father laid the matting, installed a 'Siesta' stove and knocked up a few shelves. He probably commuted from Willersey in his angry little Austin, but my mother stayed for a few weeks, sleeping on a camp bed in Madelon's room. The only lavatory was downstairs, through the mice-ridden kitchen, but we were used to chamber pots anyway. Po-cupboards always smelt a bit, whatever you did with them – hence the little bowls of potpourri, the lavender bags. 'Slops' were emptied into an enamel bucket and taken downstairs in the morning. Once, when I was pregnant, a pot broke under my weight. We thought it hilariously funny, I don't know why.

But one day at the beginning of April she packed her suitcase and was gone. We had no telephone, so in future she would communicate by constant letters, sometimes with a ten shilling note safety-pinned to the last page. I don't think it occurred to me that Madelon might miss her or feel bewildered by suddenly being alone with me in a strange place. I only remember going outside one evening after she was in bed and stroking the front wall of the cottage as though it were a cat.

4

After being looked after by women for twenty-two years I had decided that they made far too much fuss about their domestic chores, presumably because they had nothing better to do. I could make porridge and during our brief domestic life before we left for Vienna in 1938 Charles had taught me how to scramble eggs. I knew that if vegetables were put in water and boiled they became edible. I registered Madelon as a vegetarian and we lived on porridge, eggs, carrots and cheese. She continued to be a radiantly healthy child, in spite of my mother's misgivings.

In my arrogance I began writing an immense historical saga about Austria from the collapse of the Austro-Hungarian Empire in 1918 to Hitler's invasion of 1938. The protagonist, though Jewish and Viennese, managed to spend considerable time in an English country rectory, as well as fighting in the Schutzbund, helping set fire to the Ministry of Justice, defending the Karl Marx Hof, working for the Socialist underground and suffering at the hands of the Nazis. I suppose I might have been dispirited if I had known that it wouldn't be finished for another five years. As it was, I managed to work at it for at least ten minutes every day. Madelon named the typewriter my 'Busy' and on one occasion lugged it out to the vegetable patch where she did her best to bury it among the desiccated cabbages. It was an experimental, trial and error sort of life for both of us. Sometimes we were dismayed, quarrelled, burst into tears. I was constantly worried about Charles in the Blitz, and often very lonely, but on the whole those first months of independence were the happiest I had known in my grown-up life so far.

Charles came when he could. He understood how to play with Madelon, which I didn't. He rolled about on the floor, was used as a climbing frame, told stories about Mr and Mrs Beethoven and their crotchety children, ceremonially piped home Saturday's lardy cake from Mr Hatt the baker's. I was by no means grave or unduly solemn, but even as a child I had been baffled when people asked, 'Why don't you go out and play?' 'Why don't you play with your dolls?' or (worst of all) 'Why don't you go and play with so-and-so?' I was constantly changing personalities, revising my short past, creating improbable futures, but if that was a form of playing it had nothing to do with Nuts In May or Snap or putting the tail on the donkey; still less did it have anything to do with running about making a noise or throwing and failing to catch balls or being chased round the garden by some strange and possibly ferocious child.

I suspect that my mother knew how to play. Her childhood, among ten siblings, sounded a constant romp. She remembered a game inexplicably known as 'Coal-mines', in which all the furniture was pushed against the walls and you had to crawl round the room on top of it, without touching the floor. She was always the first to suggest 'Up Jenkins' or 'I Spy'. Her nieces and nephews played tennis, blind man's buff, ludo, cricket, charades, rummy, ping-pong, all things which in earlier days made me wet myself with fear, and later sent me skulking behind a book, an expression of contempt slapped askew over my abject misery. My father's rare and lugubrious attempts to 'play' bored him, let alone me, to the point of fury. The only game he could tolerate was chess, which he actually managed to teach me. I enjoyed it and never thought of it as a game, perhaps because of the grim way he played, smouldering like a volcano and slamming the pieces down as though teaching them a lesson.

Playing was only one of the things I didn't know how to do. There were many more. Making friends, for instance. If friendship was an intimate and mutually benevolent relationship independent of sexual or family love I had never experienced or even observed such a relationship. I had no idea how to recognise one, let alone make it. Occasionally men had turned up in my

13

father's life whom he said were — at last — friends, but if he made them he did it very badly, for none of them lasted more than a few weeks. ('Feet of clay' my mother would say mysteriously, I supposed in explanation.) My mother had made many friends in the past, before I could watch how she did it, but since I was expected to call them all 'Auntie' I vaguely assumed they were distant relations; in any case they seldom appeared, and weren't noticeably intimate or benevolent when they did. The only one of her friendships I observed myself was luridly described by my father as unnatural and led him to operatic demonstrations of jealousy.

Even if I had known what a friend was, I doubt if I could have made one out of 'Charlie' Jackson. Charlie lived in the large Victorian house next door and came over to investigate shortly after my mother left. Although for a while I saw a great deal of her I have only the vaguest idea what she looked like: stocky will do, with an untended complexion and wiry hair. Give her scarlet nails when she goes out to dinner, slight puffiness round the ankles, an alluring dress corrugated by corset. In the daytime she would have worn 'slacks' and a close-fitting jumper. A mariner's walk, smoked a lot, prided herself on saying what she thought. This, anyway, is the image I shall use for Charlie. It must have sprung from somewhere.

Her husband, 'Buffy', was an Army officer, though I was never clear about his rank. He seemed to live at home, in spite of the war, and was a formidable figure in his uniform, stiff, glazed, propped up on the back seat of a limousine and driven about by a perky AT. There were two sons, fierce boys aged between seven and twelve, with names like Dick and Gordon. They wore grey flannel shorts, elastic belts with snake buckles, huge black lace-up shoes; their hair was cropped, their ears like embryonic wings. They were managed, more or less, by a young woman called Smith.

The only other people to approach us were the Leversons. I can't be sure whether there was a Mr Leverson; if so, he was so old and frail that he barely existed. Mrs Leverson was tall, wild, and in a more or less permanent state of spiritual ecstasy. There was Mediterranean blood in her family: she embraced, she clasped, she wept, she laughed, her hair fell out of its bun and was skewered back anyhow, there were holes in the elbows of her cardigan and she forgot to take a bath for weeks on end. She had a daughter of about my age, a thin, nervous girl who couldn't speak without going through the most curious contortions, winding an arm round her head, standing on one leg, sinking her chin on her collarbone and bending the upper part of her body leeward as if blown by a high wind. She was a bright girl, but tiring to talk to. I don't remember her name; it could have been Romula. I knew where I was with Mrs Leverson. There were times when I even wished she would take us over, tuck us up among the crucifixes and cat shit.

Which brings me back to my mother. Perhaps the most significant memory of this time concerns her. My father was so hopelessly extravagant that she had thought it wise to keep her pitiful annuity secret and had hidden the policy with her underwear. It was her 'nest egg', the only money of her own she ever had, and supplied those ten shilling notes which she frequently safety-pinned to her letters. In one of his paranoid seizures he rummaged in her chest of drawers one afternoon while she was out 'visiting', found the policy, and in his rage actually physically injured her in some way. She left him, as far as I know for the first time in her life. I don't know whether she told me she was coming, or whether she just appeared, but she came to me.

That night I put her to bed and sat with her while she wept, pink and crumpled, into the pillow. The next morning the first of my father's letters arrived. She read it and hid it away. I kept insisting that she mustn't go back to him, but three days and three letters later she did. It was a long time before I understood why.

5

In the third week of July 1941 I discovered I was pregnant. *Over-awed by the thought, staggered by its impossibility* was the last entry in my diary for many years. I must have been thinking of the novel, for I don't remember being particularly worried about anything else. By Christmas we were back at the Rectory. I made it quite clear that our return was only temporary, but don't think my mother believed me. After a week or so everything was back to what she considered normal. She had suggested, or decided, that I had the baby in 'the spare room', a dignified bedroom next to the bathroom. It had a row of inner windows which would have overlooked the corridor if they hadn't been hung with shantung curtains. The double bedstead, very high off the ground, was mahogany. There was a profusion of porcelain ornaments, little pots and dishes and figurines. All these, for the sake of hygiene, my mother removed.

She scrubbed every inch of paint and put a large rubber sheet on the bed. I sometimes looked in apprehensively on my way to the bathroom, alarmed by the preparations more than the prospect of using them.

The baby was due at the end of March. Charles turned up for the weekend on 7th March, a Saturday. On Monday morning he didn't get up, but remained prone, apparently unconscious, in a small bedroom off the landing. I was used to him taking short holidays from life; my mother, looking in on him from time to time, said it must be 'flu. On Thursday afternoon I had my first labour pain. My mother hurried me into the spare room and Madelon next door to sympathetic neighbours. Suddenly, as I walked up and down, warm water poured out of me, odourless and far more plentiful than pee. 'Never mind,' my mother said, briskly mopping the carpet.

As in all the most notable births, there was a storm that night. Gales howled, sleet lashed the windows. The doctor was uncontactable. My mother called the District Nurse. She arrived in a round hat, examined me, muttered to my mother in a corner. She couldn't find the baby's backbone. Perhaps I was going to have a monster. 'It's Doctor's job. I can't take the responsibility,' she said primly, and bolted.

I went into the final stages of labour on the high mahogany bed, twisting and biting my mother's hand. I don't know how long it was before I began to give birth, but I clearly remember a shadow hurrying along the corridor and realising that Dr Duncan, through gale and blackout, had arrived. He gave my mother a pad soaked in chloroform to slap over my face; then with great care he pushed the mucky little foot back and wheedled the breech baby out inch by inch.

For the next week the baby lay in a bassinet on the floor. I leaned over, perilously, to change her nappies and haul her up to be fed. When Madelon was brought to see her sister she didn't say anything, but her face flushed like red ink spreading over blotting paper.

6

I don't know if it was pressure from his conscience or the Chancellor, but Charles now decided to take a job as porter at the Radcliffe Infirmary in Oxford. The four of us, suddenly become a family, moved back to The Butts. His shifts changed every week; sometimes he bicycled the five miles to Oxford at dawn and was back to take over Madelon in the afternoon; sometimes he walked her to school and pedalled away at teatime. In spite of the fact that he spent eight out of every twenty-four hours wheeling people to operating theatres, cleaning up the effusions of the dead and dying, disposing of arms, legs, wombs and other offending organs, I have the impression that he looked after Madelon and I looked after Caroline, though since he worked a forty-hour-week it couldn't actually have been so.

We must have lived like this for about a year, I can vaguely imagine it, but have only two clear memories. One day an undergraduate called Michael Fenton came to ask Charles's advice about registering as a conscientious objector. He brought a friend with him, a nervous boy, thin with a damp handshake, introduced as John

Mortimer. Charles had a bad cold and was still in his dressing gown. I left them to it, and about an hour later directed the two young men to the bus stop. The second is of sitting on the grass shelling peas and looking up to see Madelon running down the road, calling 'It's June!' In hindsight there is less reason for remembering this than there is to remember the visit of Fenton and his friend, but I have thought of it, like an anniversary, every 1st June for the last fifty years.

7

The reason for the next catastrophic decision was entirely mine. No doubt it sounded convincing. When I was nine-years-old my father, briefly fancying anthroposophy, had sent me to a Rudolf Steiner school in Streatham. I enjoyed it and when I heard about The Grange, Madelon's future education seemed solved. I went to see the headmistress, a soulful lady surrounded by nebulous water colours and folk weave, and came away with the job of 'house-mother' to fifteen children, the youngest about seven, the eldest a teenage delinquent. My payment would be Madelon's education, and bed and board for myself, Caroline and Charles, who would transfer his portering to the local hospital. In September 1943 we let The Butts to an RAF sergeant and moved in.

No doubt many of Dr Steiner's disciples are sensible and intelligent people, but The Grange was a community of crackpots. I suspect this had a great deal to do with the fact that a few weeks later Charles decided to join the Army. He had felt acceptable when he worked through the Blitz; it was the sort of thing any Oxford graduate, newspaper foreign correspondent, rowing blue, Chancellor's son, could reasonably be proud of. As a porter at the Radcliffe he at least had the justification of contributing to the well-being of his family. Now he was bicycling to the hospital every day from a crazy institution where he was supported by his wife, his intelligence offended, his opinions irrelevant. I think I was relieved by his decision. Neither of us would have believed it if some prophetic voice had told us that it meant the end of our marriage.

The Army rejected him more or less on sight; so did the Air Force. At last he was accepted by the Pioneer Corps and went away in a Private's uniform. Caroline caught pneumonia and the school's resident doctor, perfunctorily examining her, said he detected a large soul. I wrapped her in blankets, grabbed Madelon and left The Grange for ever. Since The Butts was let, we were homeless again. With my two unbaptised daughters, a typewriter and a load of tattered manuscript, I went to live with my in-laws in Salisbury Close.

CHAPTER TWO

I

Chancellor Dimont always ate his breakfast standing up: an aid, he said, to the digestion. He was a tall, solid man, invariably dressed in a cassock, with the face of a Flemish farmer and a sparse cap of silver hair. He sprinkled his cornflakes with a liberal helping of Bemax and held the plate under his chin, neatly slurping in the cereal while looking down on his seated family — his wife Norah, a little woman with alarmed eyes who constantly pinched and kneaded the edge of the tablecloth, and his three daughters, Mary, Margaret and Betty. Mary was the eldest, Betty — somewhere around my own age — the youngest. I somehow managed not to notice the sisters much. They all remained spinsters, which did them no apparent harm.

From my upstairs window I would watch my mother-in-law when she went shopping, a drear hessian bag in her gloved hand. She would scurry purposefully out of the back door, head down, squashed felt hat like a mushroom. Pause, uncertain. A moment of doubt, of dismay, then back into the house and out of sight. Two minutes later she would scuttle out again and get as far as the gate that led to the High Street, the outside world. Her hand on the latch, her squabous grey figure would stiffen. Though I couldn't see it, I knew her long nose twitched, her fingers trembled. Back she would go, muttering, shaking her head. At last, triumphantly, she would make it through the gate, closing it fussily behind her. I don't remember ever seeing her return from these expeditions. The only other thing that impressed me about her was that every night she lugged all the silver upstairs and hid it under her bed. At least that's what she told me.

Salisbury had been taken over by the American army. The great oak gates of the Close were barred at night, guarded by sentries with fixed bayonets. A Sergeant waylaid my father-in-law hurrying to Evensong: 'Excuse me, sir — who runs this joint?' 'God,' the Chancellor replied, and swept on. With my lipstick and cigarettes, sulks and enthusiasms, intractable and godless, I was not only a foreigner, but a heathen. The grief this caused my father-in-law was reserved for his prayers. He not only put up with me, but treated me with unexpected humour, courtesy and affection, which I readily returned.

Madelon went to a Dame's school and voraciously read Enid Blyton. My days must have been spent between Caroline and the typewriter, for there was a cook who seemed to fry everything except trifle, to which the family were addicted, and I don't remember doing any housework. There were soon 100,000 words of *Whom The Heavens*, and no reason why it should ever stop. Restless, bored, I took an evening job as a waitress in the American Officers' canteen. Most of the officers were very young, shiny skulls showing through the shaved stubble of hair. Sometimes one of them would walk me back to the Close gates and tell me about his life in Omaha or Missouri, his wife and kids, sweetheart or mother. There might be a respectful goodnight kiss, but that was all. The idea of loveless sex horrified me. Nevertheless I made great efforts to be sexually attractive and none whatever to be lovable. Like many other paradoxes in my life, I find this perplexing.

2

When Charles was on leave that summer he introduced me to Kenneth Harrison, a small, blonde, fastidious young man working in chemical warfare at Porton Down. Harrison recalled the event in a letter to our daughter, written nearly half a century later: ... *especially among the younger element of those who live in or floated out of the Close your mother created a stir, as it were somebody they had never seen the like of before: witty, refreshing, elegant and ... anyhow I fell in love with her, seriously, practically at first meeting. She ... began to favour me and no more needs to be said.*

I am appalled that I know so little about Harrison. His father was Chancellor of York Cathedral and he himself could assume a bland ecclesiastical air, particularly when helping my mother-in-law wind her knitting wool, or paying sly compliments to one of her daughters. He was much amused by the expurgated passages of Aubrey's *Brief Lives* and copied them out for me in his exquisite handwriting; he introduced me to Bach and Mozart and failed to convert me to Jane Austen; he had perfect pitch, was tortured by whistling. The Dimonts were delighted to look after Madelon and Caroline while we bicycled off to view parish churches. On our return

Harrison would chat to my father-in-law about tryptiches and pre-Conquest carvings.

This was long before the Pill or the coil. Many women used rubber contraptions called Dutch caps. Either you interrupted sex just as it was getting interesting, returning to it equipped but frigid, or kept the thing in, smelly and slimy as it was, until it disintegrated. I owned one for a while, but never used it. Condoms were clumsy and looked ridiculous. The only method left, apart from *coitus interruptus*, mathematics and chastity, was a dissolving pessary which could be shoved in with the minimum foresight and fuss. These were largely, if not entirely, made of cocoa butter but presumably worked more often than not, since Caroline was two-and-a-half before I became pregnant again. Julia, a pint-sized Harrison, was born on 30th March 1945. Charles was away. He assumed, as did everyone except my mother, that the baby was his. Kenneth recalled: *Naturally, we were extremely careful, and on reflexion I do not consider that anyone fathomed our real relationship, even after you were born; certainly you were registered as Penelope Julia Dimont.*

Having a daughter was perhaps the greatest event of Kenneth's life; the fact that it was a secret added to its charm. He supported her financially for many years and was a regular visitor, arriving punctually in his bowler hat and sober overcoat, stoically enduring the anarchy of children's tea, disappearing without fuss into his own mysterious world. Of all the men in my life, he was my mother's favourite.

September 6 1946: *I am nearly 28.* Johanna, *which was* Whom The Heavens Compel, *will be published by Secker and Warburg.* Holiday, *my second novel, is finished and waiting for Warburg's opinion. In October, Charles, a Captain, will be demobbed from Bad Oynehausen, B.A.O.R. At the moment we have some money. I have a Nanny for the children. I write, and may possibly become successful. We live at Willersey.*

Arturo and Ilsa Barea are in The Butts; RAF sergeants and RASC Colonels have had it and left it during the last three years. Last summer I spent six weeks there with Caroline and Julia, the happiest six weeks in the last three years. Kenneth Harrison came to stay, the present a square peg in the round hole of the past. The Butts remains the best thing that ever happened to me. Madelon wants to go back to it, not realising that everything we had then is lost. The things we have put in its place don't, I think, fill the gap. I have no idea whether it will ever be filled. Perhaps when we own something again, a house and a garden . . .

When Charles was demobilised he must have taken a room in London. I don't remember that either of us made any effort to find an alternative arrangement. The only clear memory I have of him during that time is at Willersey when Julia was about eighteen-months-old. We were sitting in front of the Siesta stove my father had installed in his old bedroom, which was now our living room. It was night, the children asleep. I told Charles that Kenneth Harrison was Julia's father. I have an impression of weeping, and don't think it was mine.

4

At the beginning of World War I my father's parish was taken over for the duration by an elderly parson and my father joined the Army as a Chaplain. My six-month-old brother Paul and our mother followed him to Woolwich, then, after he went overseas, moved between our grandmother's house in Wiltshire and various 'aunts'. Photographs show how much Paul was doted on: a chubby baby laid out in christening robes or naked on the obligatory bearskin; our father, handsome in uniform, holding him on his knee; our mother in a panama hat guiding his first steps; 'The Future Prime Minister' swaggering in a new overcoat with velvet collar. About the time I was born — possibly on the very day — Paul was sent away to boarding school. He was four-and-a-half-years-old and never lived at home again.

His anger with our parents lasted the whole of his life and his bitter resentment of me was never entirely resolved. We had a brief *rapprochement* in my teens, when he was up at Oxford, but since my marriage we had seldom met. He volunteered for the Army in 1939, transferred to the Army Film Unit and ended the war as a Lieutenant Colonel in India. A lot must have happened to him during those years, although apart from mentioning a sympathetic lady in Calcutta he never talked about it.

After he was demobilised Paul made one of his rare but significant sorties into my life. He seemed confident, rich, even playful, driving me about London at perilous speed in his new MG. He joined a documentary film company in which there were some entertaining young men in woven ties and tweed jackets, among them Laurie

Lee and Humphrey Swingler. We frequented the Gargoyle Club off Dean Street, our interesting encounters mistily reflected in the mirrored walls.

It was there that I met Randall, Humphrey's elder brother. Their father was a parson, their great-uncle had been Archbishop of Canterbury. Like Charles, even Kenneth, they displayed all the symptoms of a strict ecclesiastical background. Randall was a poet, a pre-Khrushchev communist who had won the Military Medal in the war, joined Tito's partisans when the fighting was over and ran up the Red Flag for his unit's victory parade. He looked uncannily like Jean Gabin and was married to a professional pianist, Geraldine Peppin. She lived in Essex with their young daughter and was certainly not in evidence at the Gargoyle.

I didn't realise it at the time, but Kenneth had controlled our relationship: concern and responsibility up to a certain point, beyond that unknown territory, impractical and unwise to enter. This may have meant 'falling in love' to him, but to me it was little more than a pleasant occupation, lacking the romantic upheaval that in those days I thought necessary to sex. I fell passionately in love with Randall. He put up a faint struggle – less, I think, to do with conscience than lack of confidence – but I won him over, anyway for a while.

Neither of us were content with furtive weekends, even if we could have afforded them. In one of my many periods of mistaking myself for someone else I had taken on a dramatisation of the country's economic situation for radio, and with working on this as an implausible excuse rented a cottage hung with cobwebs and dead herbs on Southend Common near Henley-on-Thames. Julia remained at Willersey with my mother; Caroline, then five-and-a-half, joined Madelon at boarding school for the autumn term — much to her fury, she would stay there for the next two years. Randall commuted between Southend Common, his home in Essex and his London pad. He was constantly on the move.

If, as I've recorded, the second time I met John Mortimer was on 30th November it must have been a very prolonged Indian summer that year. I was painting a coal scuttle in the garden and looked up to see a horse looming over the hedge. After a moment's alarm I noticed a young man in glasses sitting on the horse. Presumably he introduced himself, saying he lived nearby with his parents and was a friend of Randall's. I told him I'd run out of bread. He offered to fetch me bread, and trotted away.

5

I was twenty-nine, Randall in his late thirties. My impression is that our affair was a solemn business, needing constant analysis, and that John, at twenty-four, provided a welcome diversion. I remember all three of us walking across Turville Heath, Randall and I staggering, hysterical with laughter, at the Mortimer impersonation of an old, testy barrister. I knew John was reading for the Bar, but hadn't yet met his father and had no idea of the significance of this hilarious pantomime. His generic term for everything he enjoyed was 'Sprat' and he pursued what Sprat there was round Turville Heath Common with desperate fervour. He was a clever, skinny, excitable youth — a more apt description, actually, than 'young man' — and I enjoyed being taken to pubs where he was treated indulgently as the young Squire, a bit of a lad, always ready for a bottle of scotch or can of black market petrol.

It would be absurd to pretend that I knew — or know — why he fell in love with me. My belief is that he was virtually inexperienced with women and that the girl-friends he told me about, if not exactly figments of his imagination, were much embellished by it. He certainly had two clear fantasies, neither of which had anything to do with me. The first was of a bouncing, good natured semi-boy, slightly grubby, always ready for a lark. Perhaps the girl he called 'Cornish Pasty' (her name was Patsy?) was one of these. The second was of high heels busily tapping to work in some executive office. Siriol Hugh-Jones, who worked on *Vogue*, must have come into this category. I first met her when she was staying the weekend in his parents' house. Although she could only have been in her mid-twenties, it was impossible to think of her as a 'girl'. She was a witty, gallant little woman, wearing a skirt that showed the faded mark of last year's hemline. I liked her enormously, and later she became the only close friend I ever had.

When Randall was away for the night, which was frequently, John would collect me in his father's ancient, formidable car and we would sit on bar stools lengthily considering the advisability of his marriage to one or other of these candidates. I tended to plump for 'Cornish Pasty', perhaps because I'd never met her. I talked a great deal about myself too, since he was an eager audience. What was fairly commonplace to me — love affairs, marriage, children, writing — may have seemed exotic to an only child with an immediate past of

Brasenose and Harrow. No need for caution, anyway. One night he stopped the car on a bumpy track over the Common and said in a practical voice, 'What about a quick fuck and then home?' I was astounded but stopped myself laughing, thinking that perhaps some more serious need was trying to speak out. I would learn in time that this need was my own and that I would almost always be mistaken in attributing it to John. He drove on philosophically, no offence taken, but from then on I made much of 'being an aunt' to him, the only time in my life I have attempted to play this role.

6

Before very long I was pregnant again — plain bloody carelessness my brother said. I arranged to meet Randall in the bar of the Gargoyle. He was late. I sat next to Dylan Thomas. It must have been winter, but I was wearing a sleeveless dress or blouse. With his stubby, nicotine-stained fingers, Thomas played 'Insy-winsy-spider' up and down my bare arm:

> Insy-winsy spider
> climbed up the water spout...
> Down came the rain
> and washed the spider out...
> OUT came the sun and dried up all the rain
> Insy-winsy spider
> climbed up the spout again...

And again. It was soothing. When Randall arrived I told him calmly, almost by the way, that I was pregnant. My memory, which may not be totally correct, tells me that he got up and left immediately. Whether that's so or not,

I didn't see him again for seventeen years. I packed up the cottage and went back to Willersey.

I know there must have been a time of mourning. I had understandably been sacked from the radio job; this didn't distress me, but on the other hand I wasn't writing anything and the prospect of an indefinite period at Willersey with no one to talk to, nothing to do but compete with my mother over Julia, was appalling. Two years before, Kenneth had given me a car, an Austin of some sort, which I had learned to drive by driving, frequently backwards and almost always into something. By now it was little more than an engine on wheels, perilously surrounded by bits of chassis, but it provided a means of escape. I dressed Julia in her Daniel Neal overcoat with velvet collar and took her to stay with the Mortimers for the weekend.

Clifford Mortimer had built Turville Heath Cottage before he went blind. It was a perfect period piece and might well have been on the cover of an early 1930s issue of *Ideal Home* — steep pantiled roof, metal window frames, white clap-board. Indoors smelt of wood smoke and paraffin, the furniture was bleached oak from Heals, the polished floors scattered with rugs of homespun design. There was an Austrian cook called Hansi who lived in a dark little room off the kitchen and was ribald with John. Upstairs were three bedrooms and a tiny bathroom, all heated by paraffin stoves. Julia and I were put in the middle bedroom. Early morning tea was served with bread and butter and there was a canister of dry biscuits for nibbling during the night. I certainly wasn't in love with John at that time, but comforted by his attention and enjoyed his company. Against all my high-flown principles about loveless sex I found myself tip-toeing into his room, leaving Julia soundly asleep. Whatever else he may have felt, I know he was amazed.

7

My mother was appalled by my pregnancy, but resigned. John, who had sophisticated friends, said of course I must have an abortion — he had been told of a woman in Chelsea who would do it for a reasonable fee. I had and always have had an instinctive horror of abortion, though fervently supporting it in principle. Another baby didn't seem to me to present any grave problem; on the other hand maybe it was time to conform and be 'sensible' for once. I agreed to let John take me to the woman for a preliminary interview, but remember nothing about her. All I remember is bolting out of her house and running down the street, John following and calling out 'What's wrong? What's the matter?'

Charles had just been admitted to a psychiatric hospital in the Midlands, presumably to dry out. I was genuinely worried that he had nowhere to go when the treatment was finished. In the Spring of 1948 the three children and I moved from Willersey and crammed into an olde worlde one-and-a-half up and one down commuter's dream in Turville, found for us by John and intended as a convalescent home for my husband. Charles arrived, stayed for a few days, disappeared again. We must have agreed not to resume 'marital relations' — he slept, I remember, in a kind of cupboard off the half-bedroom —

but I don't think we quarrelled, or that there were any recriminations. It may have been then that he offered to assume the unborn baby's paternity. I accepted the offer, grateful for his concern even though I didn't really see it was necessary.

Every Friday evening, changed from his city gear into corduroys, leather elbow-patches on a newish tweed jacket, (all his clothes came from Hall Bros. in Oxford, though Hansi made some of his silk shirts), John would walk down the hill, across the fields with gibbeted blackbirds hanging from gamekeepers' scaffolds, through the woods, arriving in a state of over-excited exhaustion to grapple with me as I cooked or washed up or persuaded the children to bed. We had parties, full of people I didn't know. My brother was staying for one of them. At some point I came into the sitting room, where he was lying on the sofa. I was rumpled, covered in strands of hay. He looked at me despondently. 'You are a chump,' he said.

Possibly as a consequence of an over-active sex life I started labour two months early, summoned my mother and drove myself into Henley. Randall's daughter Deborah, weighing slightly over four pounds and with a quantity of red hair, was born in a couple of hours to the accompaniment of *Great Expectations* read aloud by a burly midwife. Six weeks later John and I took her to Ireland. We stayed one night in Dublin, then set out to drive to Connemara, getting lost after dark in an endless expanse of bog, the petrol gauge inching to zero, Deborah apoplectic.

The following Sunday we went for a walk, leaving the infant in her travel cot by the open window. The village

33

was deserted. No doubt I was fussing about the time — this was long before the days of feeding 'on demand' and being so puny Deborah was fed every three hours. As we walked back we could hear her wails gathering strength in the distance. The door was locked, everyone had gone to Mass. After a few ineffectual attempts to climb in we sat on the harbour wall and waited. The wails changed key, became frantic. My shirt was soaked with milk, Deborah choking, struggling for breath. I don't remember raging, but it would have been in character. If John had been able to recognise it he might have seen for the first time what he was letting himself in for. He didn't. My life may have seemed to him full of such enviable dramas.

8

A few months later we rented a sort of seaside house — thin doors that banged in the wind, weeds, rubble — in a village not far from Turville Heath and John came to live with us. To Clifford Mortimer, the woman and children for whom his son left home must have been at first little more than voices, mine reluctant and almost inaudible, the rest a ragged chorus of chatter and wails. Before long he seemed to grow used to disturbance, which normally he detested, and knew the size and weight of the children as they sprawled on his knee, pried in his waistcoat pocket for the gold Albert which magically sprung open when blown on.

Perhaps the most extraordinary thing about the whole bizarre situation was the old man's tolerance of it. Or was it just that he couldn't be bothered? That's quite possible, with so many more important things to fret about — earwigs and greenfly, the cost of oysters, the maddening inefficiency of waiters, the laggardliness of his wife in coming to tie his shoe laces, the absurdities of Probate, Divorce and Admiralty. When he castigated his son, which was frequently, I don't think it was because of John's unsuitable liaison so much as his ineffectual performance. I remember sitting on the lawn at Turvillle Heath feeling protective and angry as I listened through an open window to the old man's bellows occasionally interrupted by moments of silence, which I supposed were John's mumbling defence. Whatever these rows were about they remained private, part of an exclusive relationship, and were never referred to by any of us. Both parents, while in their way fiercely loving, seemed to regard their only child as something of a joke. The one thing they said they didn't understand was how a woman like myself, with a car and furniture, could see anything in him.

John's mother, Kathleen, was an innocent, secretive woman. Her blind husband scorned any attempt at independence apart from learning Braille in order to read Shakespeare's sonnets, and at first sight she seemed no more than a devoted shadow, always hovering to supply his demands, reading his briefs outloud, sitting behind him in court ready to help if his memory failed (which it never did), cutting up his food, walking him round the garden describing each plant, tree and shrub. Her relationship with the rest of the world, including John, consequently seemed remote, something which she observed with interest but didn't actually experience.

The first time I saw another side to her was one

afternoon when I was sitting in their garden, reading or writing, one eye on the children. Clifford and Kathleen, arm in arm, had started their usual slow walk along the path between the borders, he with his stick and tweed hat, she in her baggy cardigan, her hair loosening from its bun, a shapeless, neutral figure. Suddenly I heard the old man bellow 'Kath!' as though in terrible danger. Kathleen had detached herself and walked alone to the brink of the lawn, where it sloped down to the valley. She stood there, arms folded, on the horizon. Clifford, bereft and helpless, yelled 'Kath! Kath!', but she didn't move. Neither did I. He was blundering about, roaring, waving his stick, lost. In her own time Kathleen turned and walked leisurely back, took his arm and calmly continued her description of the dahlias. Perhaps these rare but ruthless truancies were in preparation for the time when she would be left alone — it was unthinkable that she should die first. If so, they served her well; after the initial devastation of his death she was able to collect herself and look at what was left of her life with a mild, enquiring eye and shockingly cool judgement.

9

Over the next eighteen months I fell in love. Perhaps the fact that it happened to be with John was something Fate ordained the day he chose to come to The Butts with Michael Fenton, or long before that in some wayward calculation of the stars. Perhaps (and I think it more likely) it was just a matter of chance: another place, another season, and I might have met an agreeable forty-year-old who would have taken my father's advice and kept a hand on my tiller. Even better — infinitely better — I might have told myself that I was thirty-years-old, with four children, and that it was time to take stock of my life and change direction. Such speculations are pointless, though in idle moments, sleepless nights, they may serve to pass the time. The fact was that I fell in love with John.

'Why?' people ask. If I chose to believe the whole thing fortuitous I could answer 'Because he was there,' but that wouldn't be entirely — perhaps not even minimally — true. Nevertheless I approach other explanations with caution. I could say that he appealed to the child in me, or the woman who had never grown up; that I played his forbidden games, shared many of his secrets, relished his sense of naughtiness; that I was at the same time a permissive mother allowing him through the locked door, where games were all the more fun for their spice of incest. Most of that may be true, as far as it goes. There was also the fact that he was talented, funny, spoiled me in many ways — breakfast in bed, cosseting, treats, presents — and was remarkably tolerant of the children. I could go on, but it would be fiction. Apart from my mother, he has undoubtedly been the most influential person in my life.

I'm not sure when marriage began to seem a serious possibility. John proposed it for a long time, without any great conviction, but I still felt an illogical responsibility for Charles. One morning, however, I received the classic letter — 'By the time you receive this ...' — which resulted in a panic drive to the Fulham Hospital where I found a buxom girl called Sonia sitting on my husband's deathbed slapping his face, briskly chanting 'Wakey,

wakey!' The relief was perhaps a little bleak, but from then on I knew he was in good hands.

Shortly after this John and I met for lunch at the Queen's Hotel in Sloane Square. Over the sole veronique he said, 'If you marry me you'll have thirty acres.' I had no conception of thirty acres. On the other hand perhaps I felt I was being offered something more than John himself; perhaps I was momentarily reconciled to old age. I don't think I accepted the offer in so many words, but it seems that from then on the idea of marriage took its own momentum and became inevitable.

There were minor difficulties. Charles, restored, inexplicably found moral objections to divorcing me. These were somehow overcome, but then our efforts to prove adultery were ineffective – chambermaids were uncooperative, and even our dressing gowns hanging on the same peg didn't impress the private detective who came at considerable expense to smell out sin. Finally, however, the authorities were convinced that I was an unfaithful wife. One summer evening I walked down to meet John at the 'bus stop. Perhaps I was a few minutes late, because he was already coming up the hill. 'You're a free woman,' he said. He looked rather sick and wasn't smiling.

The night before my wedding to Charles, ten years before, I had shared a hotel bedroom with my mother. After she tucked herself up I sat brushing my hair and saw in the mirror that she was gazing at me with an expression of infinite pity. 'To think,' she said, 'that tomorrow night you will be *sharing a bed*!' She chose to overlook the fact that I had been living with Charles for some months – it was marriage that appalled her, the prospect of lifelong intimacy. Since then she had connived at my relationships with Kenneth and Randall and taken over their children with delight. Either she had grown more cynical or finally given me up as hopeless, but whatever she thought of my marrying John, she kept quiet about it. We went shopping for a wedding costume as though I were a virginal eighteen-year-old and her four grand-daughters hopes for the distant future. For some reason we ended up at a dress shop in Park Lane, though the image of my mother in Park Lane is bizarre. I bought a muted tartan skirt, a brown velvet jacket with muted tartan collar and cuffs and a sort of doge's hat. I like to think that after this I took her to tea in Fortnums, but that may be what I wish I had done.

John and I were married at Chelsea Register Office on 27th August 1949, the day my divorce to Charles was made Absolute. As both our parents attended, I have no idea who was looking after the children; or, indeed, why the children weren't there. We had a party in the Mortimers' flat at 11, King's Bench Walk, which from now on would be our home. The last stragglers were virtually pushed out of the door towards dawn and we went to St Malo for a three-day honeymoon.

10

The flat was on the fourth floor of 11 King's Bench Walk, overlooking the Middle Temple garden where there is a statue bearing the consoling legend LAWYERS WERE CHILDREN ONCE. It consisted of a large living room still redolent of port and cigars, a bedroom, and a sizeable cupboard with a window. Bathroom and kitchen had ingeniously been fitted into a narrow corridor. Caroline was brought home from boarding school and shared the bedroom with Julia and Randall's fifteen-month-old daughter Deborah. Barristers on the floor below were maddened by the frenzied creaking of the rocking horse, solicitors in the basement complained about soapsuds in the drain. John and I slept in the cupboard, which exactly fitted a double bed; we dressed and undressed on a sort of trampoline. When our daughter Sally was born she spent her days by the cupboard window, her nights in the living room under a festoon of drying nappies.

When John had been called to the Bar in 1948 he had joined his father's Chambers in Dr Johnson's Buildings and shared his father's murky room. Now, although he was still an active barrister, Clifford began to leave the tedious, subsidiary work to his son and come up to London less often, consequently John often had the room to himself. It fascinated me and constantly appeared in my dreams. The life he led there, though only a few hundred yards from our flat, seemed mysterious, obscurely threatening. The Chief Clerk was called Charlie, but from long tradition was known as George. The hat-stands were hung with grey, curled scalps. Unimaginable brutalities and perversions lurked inside briefs tied in chewed pink ribbon. When I went there my familiar husband seemed strange, clammy, over-anxious. His barrister's uniform smelled of sweat, semen and cologne.

Neither of us had seriously considered the financial situation. As far as I remember Clifford gave John the flat rent free and an allowance of five pounds a week. My children had survived so far on faith, hope and a great deal of charity; I supposed this was how we would continue and in some miraculous way we did. Madelon was at boarding school, ostensibly paid for by Charles, my mother provided their clothes and had most of them to stay in the holidays, Kenneth supported Julia and to some extent subsidised me. He also gave us Burnt House Farm in Essex to use for weekends and holidays and an enormous Ford V8 station wagon to get there in. The children remember keeping white mice in the barn, I remember John changing Sally's nappy on the kitchen table, John cutting Julia's hair round the rim of a pudding basin. He enjoyed the novel game of domesticity, cooked and cleaned and would have made an excellent mother. Masculine jobs such as starting the electric generator, putting up shelves or cutting the grass depressed him enormously. 'Get a man in' became one of those family sayings that can be applied to almost anything.

12

We lived in King's Bench Walk for nearly three years, but only fragments of that time survive: I stand at the sitting room window, watching. Late, always late, he comes through the archway at the top of the car park and walks down towards Number 11, head down, briefcase bumping against his leg. He doesn't know I am watching and I don't know what he's thinking. For these few minutes we are alone in separate worlds. There are parties, New Look girls in cowpat hats, long skirts and waspies, dishevelled young men being sick in the bathroom. At weekends we sometimes take the children for walks in the deserted City; Caroline may even ride her bicycle up Fetter Lane. We hear and watch the Festival of Britain being built on the other side of the river. In the evenings I type Undefendeds and Discretion Statements, bewildered by both. Sometimes we meet for lunch in the sepulchral Law Courts; his parents are there, 'Is there any danger of getting something to eat?' Clifford demands, glaring blindly about. We all have two birthdays. We make love, we quarrel, we make it up, we quarrel, we make it up, we make love.

CHAPTER THREE

1

Early in 1952 we swapped the freehold of Burnt House Farm for the last seven years of the lease of a house in Harben Road, Swiss Cottage. This is the point where memory begins to focus. Though distant and still largely obscured by the future, I begin to recognise myself.

After the austerity of The Temple, Swiss Cottage seemed cosmopolitan and glamorous. There was a shop on the corner of Goldhurst Terrace that sold nothing but coffee; the smell of roasting coffee beans started outside the Dorice Restaurant (*gullasch, nockerl, Wiener Gugel-hupf*) and drifted down into Finchley Road tube station. There were delicatessens and patisseries, a huge Odeon cinema with a Wurlitzer. Most impressive of all, there was John Barnes.

John Barnes was a branch of the John Lewis Partnership. No doubt it was called John Barnes after some dignified draper. We would become familiar with the match-seller who stood year after year in front of the entrance; we would get to know the assistants' names; they would enquire after our children and dogs, we followed the progress of their failing mothers, commiserated with them if they had colds or unsympathetic landlords. One of the children's greatest treats would be tea in the restaurant, small metal teapots that burned your fingers, fishpaste and cress sandwiches, chocolate éclairs served by tired, kindly women in little pinafores and frilled caps. When we first started going there in the early fifties they still packed your money into metal cylinders sent trundling on cables to the cash desk, but Partnership On The Scale Of Modern Industry soon introduced cash registers which opened and shut with a satisfactory ting of a bell. The place was musical with these bells. There was a food department down in the basement. At first it had counters, assistants in white cotton coats weighing out tea, cutting cheeses with wire; later it was turned into a supermarket, but never lost its air of reverence. There was haberdashery – tape and elastic, bales of bias binding, Sylko in any shade of any colour you needed, dress-making shears, very small scissors, their blades fashioned like a stork's beak – and a shoe department in which the children would be bought crepe-soled sandals and peer at their weird black bones in the x-ray machine. The Partnership got rid of the x-ray machine and cheered up Fashions, which until then had consisted of sombre dresses, sturdy coats and skirts, pink corsets and melancholy blouses. By the mid-sixties John Barnes had become part of our lives, our village green and market place.

23, Harben Road had a peppercorn rent and though I suppose there were rates we had eight rooms, a hallway, stairs, landings and passages for virtually nothing. The sitting room, in which I was to spend a great deal of my time for the next thirteen years, was the width of the house and had tall sash windows looking down over our garden and the neighbouring gardens. In the front there was a large, gloomy dining room with a service lift that could be clanked up from the basement kitchen; this was the nursery until we became prosperous, when it was converted into a kitchen and the nursery moved down to garden level. The other room on that level was a dungeon, its window facing the retaining wall of the front garden. Over the years, like many other rooms, it continually changed its purpose, ending up as John's study; but I remember my mother slept there occasionally and at times it was taken over by 'helps' too superior or elderly to climb the stairs to the attics. This basement with its dark passage, cupboard stacked with children's outgrown shoes, rickety shelves piled with old saucepans and chipped china, broken dolls' prams, bits of bicycle, dead radios, would be a recurring trauma for the rest of my life, a symbol of the subterranean chaos I longed to straighten out.

To begin with we all slept in the three bedrooms on the first floor where the rooms were light, the ceilings high. There was only one small bathroom, but we didn't seem to find it inadequate in spite of the confusion of toothbrushes, face flannels and rubber toys. The attic rooms changed ownership over the years. At first one of them was occupied by a lodger, a young man with the memorable name of Oliver Stallybrass; then teenagers, starting with Madelon, took over, and were joined by the more sprightly Mother's Helps. These rooms had tiny windows and sloping ceilings. Like the adolescents who lived in them they were remote, removed from the commotion in the house below.

John and I painted the hall dark red and moved in our scanty furniture. There was no central heating; coal had to be carried from the basement bunker for the sitting room fire and there were paraffin heaters which smelled powerfully and were, I suppose, dangerous. During our first winter fog stuck to the windowsills and we could see our breath indoors. I loved the house always, and never blamed it for anything that happened there.

2

Johanna and John's first novel, *Charade* had been published more or less at the same time, soon after we met. *Charade* was an instant success but *Johanna* died at birth – the only place it was ever mentioned, as far as I know, was in Fred Warburg's autobiography. He turned down my second book with the advice that I should go away and read the history of the Peloponnesian War; I had written nothing since. By 1952 John was working on his fifth novel. That summer Sally, now a benign two-year-old, and Deborah stayed with his parents and we took Madelon, Caroline and Julia to a dilapidated bungalow on an island in the Thames. Since they could more or less look after themselves I carried my typewriter and an old card table to the river bank and for the first time in seven years started to write a book.

I don't remember much about *A Villa In Summer* except that it had a rather sickly happy ending. However, I was working again, and some sort of help became necessary. When the holidays were over I found Mrs Medway, an indefatigable little woman who lugged coal and scrubbed floors and took away a dead canary for Catholic burial. She would see our unborn son go to boarding school, Sally become a teenager, Julia and

Caroline leave home; in her last years with us she brought me breakfast in bed half-a-mile away, then scurried back to Harben Road to clean up for John. She used to talk to my mother quite a bit, but during all that time I don't remember that she ever made one comment to me or expressed an opinion, except about the canary.

Work was by no means a priority. I spent a lot of time making clothes for the children and myself on the small, chain-stitch Singer machine my mother had been given as a wedding present in 1910: one mistaken snip and the whole thing unravelled. I had a dressmaker's dummy with flat, gently sloping bosom and hips, amputated at the crotch, tightly covered in some sort of ticking; the carpet was always scattered with bits of thread, scraps of material and trodden-on chalk. When I had collected Deborah and Sally from nursery school and Caroline and Julia were back bursting with the injustices of their day we would have tea: bread and butter and a repulsive goo called chocolate spread, Lyons cup cakes. At six o'clock sharp I would start putting the smaller children to bed, balancing my gin-and-orange on the edge of the bath, listening for John's key in the lock. In those days the older ones always went to bed, or at least disappeared, soon after he got back. The evenings were ours.

We didn't have television for years; when we finally got one it was kept in the nursery and seemed to show nothing but Dr Who and Magic Roundabout. John worked, chewing the end of the pink tape that tied his briefs; I darned socks, sewed on buttons, incessantly let down and took up hems. Sometimes when the children were asleep we carelessly went to the pub or even walked up to the last show at the Odeon. At weekends John might take Caroline and Julia riding or we piled into a motor launch at Henley and chugged up the river past stockbrokers' lawns and willows, islands where people in dark glasses lounged on the decks of houses built like paddle steamers.

Something more needs to be said about these early years at Harben Road. I scrabble and search, but don't know what I'm looking for. We were in love, ambitious, and in charge of five children: those are the things that motivated our lives. If we thought of the future at all, it was as a glamorised extension of the present. Very often they conflicted. There were dramatic quarrels, passionate reconciliations. We went to Paris for a weekend – presumably my mother took charge – and a fortune-teller in the Place du Théâtre told John that he wouldn't find true happiness until he was fifty. I was dreadfully distressed by this, but didn't say so. I changed Caroline's, Julia's and Deborah's surname from Dimont to Mortimer. They were pleased, though complaining that they came lower down in the alphabet.

There were a lot of friends and parties, dancing to 78s of Bing Crosby and Rosemary Clooney, Charles Trenet singing 'Chanson des Rues', Fats Waller's 'My Very Good Friend the Milkman', Louis Armstrong's 'Georgia'. I try to recall these friends, but few of them have names, let alone faces: Humphrey Swingler, Derek Hart, Siriol Hugh-Jones and her sister Small, James Michie and a wife called Daphne, the ebullient Moyra Fraser, Wolf and Ann Mankowitz (Julia would marry their eldest son); the novelist William Sansom and his wife Ruth, who told me she longed for her baby boy to be homosexual because homosexuals were so good to their mothers; Michael Fenton, who had visited The Butts so long ago, soon to blow his brains out after shooting his mistress ... They were all in their late twenties or early thirties. Blessed or cursed with a more or less ageless appearance, I kept quiet while they talked about thirty-five as though it were a date of distant execution.

CHAPTER FOUR

It may be possible in hindsight to see how one thing led to another, multiplied, split, took many different directions, formed an inextricable tangle with the beginning forgotten and the end (which might unravel the whole thing?) impossible to find; but it would be tedious and unrewarding to track back inch by inch in order to reconstruct it all accurately. The result would be exactly the same. Let what happens seem fortuitous, change inexplicable — that's how it is when you're living it.

A Villa In Summer was published in 1954 under the guise of a first novel; I agreed to this without a pang for the years spent struggling with the history of the Austro-Hungarian Empire. Its reviews bewildered me, and still do: 'a brilliantly successful attack on one of the most challenging fortresses of fiction: the spiritual and physical relationship of married life. Masterly in its technical skill and imaginative truth' and so on. In my own estimation it was all right; far from anything I hoped to do in the future, but just about all right.

On publication day Michael Joseph took me to lunch at the Caprice, which seemed to me like a Roman camp with its braziers and silver and hundredweights of flowers. Did I, he asked, want to be a commercial success or a serious writer? Both, apparently, were possible. He had named a racehorse after Monica Dickens; I was tempted by the idea of winning the Derby someday. Charles and Oona Chaplin were sitting at the next table and the waiter momentarily mistook me for Audrey Hepburn. Such glamour and attention were irresistible (at the age of twelve I had written a poem resisting it: 'Falsely, falsely plucking at my sleeve with lacquered fingers', it began, stern Methodist stuff). In the morning John had given me a little china house, Villa at the beginning of summer, festooned with lilac, a swain and his lass standing primly on either side of the doorway.

2

That summer we rented a prep school in Swanage, installed my parents and the children and drove to Rome and back. I crashed the car in Switzerland, we staggered over the Simplon with a broken exhaust and a leaking radiator, a mechanic slowly and methodically took our engine to pieces in Lirice. I conceived our son in Besançon, as far as we were concerned the most memorable thing about that ancient city.

Jeremy was born the following April. I was in a pleasant haze of gas and air when for the sixth time in my life I asked 'Boy or girl?' They told me, but I thought I hadn't heard right and asked again. 'A boy,' they said patiently, 'A lovely baby boy.' I didn't believe them. When we were alone in my room I braced myself and reluctantly unpinned my sixth daughter's nappy. 'It's a boy!' I yelled on the 'phone. 'Stale buns,' some child said scornfully, 'Dad told us hours ago.' John wrote to me the next day: *Now we've got a boy at last, got everything we can ever deserve or want, we must enjoy our luck. I am consumed with longing for the great excitements, a future containing a few bull fights, some dark olés, a cold, not too comfortable Spanish hotel ... I long for some great adventure, to start out with you for somewhere very old and distant, to know that our son is growing up, every day older ...*

Unfortunately the joy and pride we felt in Jeremy wasn't something we could stand on the mantelpiece or pin up in the loo. Instead of the relative freedom of the past four years there were broken nights, nappies, feeds. I was harassed, dull company, trying to write another novel, reluctant even to go to the pub. John, who had spent the greater part of his twenties being a husband, father and step-father, was restless, uneasy about wasted time and opportunities. If I knew this (and I suspect I did), it wasn't anything I could face up to, let alone do anything about. He began coming home later, making furtive 'phone calls, being extravagantly affectionate for no reason. When he finally told me he was having an affair – though I doubt whether it was much more than an interesting flirtation – my grief bewildered him. All my life I had been used to absolute power, exclusive attention. Who was I, if I wasn't unique? No one I could recognise. John was correct in saying I was like someone who had lost an empire. I fixed the pieces of my self-esteem together in some semblance of the original, but the image was never quite the same.

It was about then we discovered 'uppers'. Doctors in the Fifties, even the most highly-principled like our own GP, handed out pep pills without a qualm. The only effect they appeared to have on John was slightly to increase his normal state of agitation, but I felt they supplied something I lacked that other women presumably had — frivolity, the ability to adapt, to take life as others found it After Jeremy, Sally and Deborah were settled for the night we left Caroline in charge and raced off to parties or clubs. When we got home I could work most of the night, grabbing an hour or two of uneasy sleep before Jeremy's first feed and the general exodus; another pill and I worked till mid-afternoon, with a couple of intervals for the baby. Necessary shopping was done on the way to fetch the others from school, then, with the longed-for yet dreaded sound of John's key in the lock, another pill and the whole thing started again.

Something like a Safety Curtain slammed down, trapping me on the wrong side. One morning I woke to find I couldn't get out of bed. John, dismayed and anxious, 'phoned the doctor, dealt with the children, and by that evening a trained Nanny had taken over. I didn't see her for some days, but was told she was tall, blonde, German, wore a starched apron and cuffs and was called Helga. I heard her moving about the landing, going up and downstairs, knew she was carrying Jeremy, bathing and dressing him, talking to him. Bitterly jealous, wonderfully relieved, I stayed in hiding.

It was assumed I was just 'in the dumps' and that a

holiday would put me right. Igls, in the Austrian Alps, was chosen as a bracing spot. Caroline was taken out of school to come with me; Helga and the rest of the children went to stay with John's wealthy Aunt Daisy. For the first time in seven years John was left alone. He wrote to me every day with news of the children and messages of encouragement; I replied telling him about the people we met on the ski slopes, Caroline hurtling intrepidly down mountains. After we returned home it was arranged that I should see a Dr Fieldman, who might be able to raise my spirits. Dr Fieldman was a classic Freudian, very small, with a neat moustache. My sense of the ridiculous, the only part of me that seemed to have survived more or less intact, got in the way. As far as Dr Fieldman was concerned I was a failure.

Helga stayed on, miraculously placid with the children, devoted to Jeremy and amused, rather than irritated, by us. I have always been vulnerable to mother-figures, insatiably greedy to be cared for, and Helga was the first of many young women who more or less adequately filled the gap. Unfortunately the adult in me resented this dependence. All I could write was 'women's' journalism, which I detested and therefore found appallingly difficult. Unable to tell the truth as I saw it — how the vast majority of people jostle their way along like people in a rush hour towards some very vague destination, gently or savagely pulling their children along behind them, glancing down occasionally to see if they're still there — I invented artificial problems and solutions which at any rate fooled the editors. Working at this rubbish, no longer certain of John, distanced from the children by the admirable Helga, I raced to the notebook:

54

March 26 1956: *I sit stiffly in uncomfortable clothes drinking gin and Dubonnet. It's quarter past six in the evening, for the first time the window is wide open at the bottom; scores of birds twitter, whistle, bustle in the trees; this morning the German* gartenfrau *was hosing her plants as though it were already summer. The thought of summer coming is very comforting. The autumn, however prosperous and happy our life, is full of foreboding. One recognises sounds: birds & traffic and last night someone playing Land of Hope and Glory on the piano.*

The house is full. Madelon and Caroline downstairs; probably the wireless is on in their hot little den. I'm not sure whether 'den' is right, but somewhere where animals & heat & darkness live. Upstairs Jeremy, Sally, Deborah. A lax umbilical cord goes from this chair along the hall and up the stairs and through the rickety bars of his cot. I feel it and he doesn't. The other two pound about, hitting the floor with their still shapeless feet. On this level Julia, with blacked face and strange fancy dress, with Judy, her occasional friend.

If only one lived in another age, if only everything wasn't imprisoned in this body, belted and covered and clamped and sitting upright in a hard armchair.

After that there's no more to say. I would like to write for hours but there isn't any more, so I'll get up and hobble somewhere, upstairs or down, in my tight skirt; apologise to the children.

CHAPTER FIVE

My so-called second novel, *The Bright Prison*, disappointed Michael Joseph. I think he felt that I might be succumbing to cynicism and gloom, neither of which would buy a race horse. Anyway he was concerned, and with reckless generosity sent us to Positano for the summer of 1956 to write a book about living abroad with children. Helga came with us, making nine people of varying sizes. Our house, owned by a lugubrious painter called Peter Ruta, was little more than four small caves in the hillside; we swarmed through it, dizzy with heat and Chianti and the difficulty of buying cornflakes. Both John and I kept diaries, though his was a good deal more meticulous and useful to the book than mine, which is so blotched with Ambre Solaire that it is even harder to decipher than memory.

We adopted Fornillo beach, which was too small and insanitary for most people. Umbrellas stood along the sea's edge like a sparse herbaceous border and Salvatore, the waiter who said he was related to Frank Sinatra, spread check tablecloths under the vines. The children centred their lives round the band at Da Puppeto's, made up of students from Naples University. Peppino, who was Madelon's, played elaborate boogie on the tinny piano, the others sat round him with expressions of grave respect. An Italian film actress scampered across the stones with her middleaged lover. Like many Italian women she was within a moment of being a dwarf and wore a flowerpot hat; looking down over the barricade of her bust she must have been unable to see her feet. The piano rolled like treacle, sweet as sea-sickness. Julia hung her plaits out to dry, grinned, sparkled, danced on the hot stone. They played 'I'm in the Mood for Love' and her bare feet tapped and the band went into a morning ecstasy.

Jay Deiss — I believe he wrote a book called *Washington Story* — and his wife invaded the beach. He was a good-looking man who aimed himself at conversation like a knife at a target. Their sixteen-year-old son Casey canoed in, a lean, brown, spectacled boy carrying a few shreds of seaweed he had pulled from rocks seventy feet down. His mother said, 'Casey, I don't like you going that deep.' He answered coldly, 'I think tomorrow I can do a hundred,' and added that his nose had begun to bleed down there. Deiss said, 'First your nose begins to bleed, then your brains stream out through your nose, that is really interesting.' I made a quick sound of disgust and he grinned, pleased that he had disgusted me. Julia much admired Casey with his muscular wet suit and his knives. Like his father, he was an arrow or blade, hardly human.

There were no telephones in Positano in those days. In the afternoons, when all the shutters were closed and the beaches deserted, small boys would dawdle up and down carrying notes of invitation, instruction, gossip, abuse or love. The first of these we received was from Phyllis, Peter Ruta's current mistress: there was a party at Nerano, everyone would be there, would we like to go with them? Of course, but what to wear? It was long before jeans were *de rigueur* and most women in Positano dressed like entrants to a beauty contest, tight jumpers with plunging necklines, tight silk pedal-pushers, high heels, jewellery. I must make a dress. I feverishly tore one out while John went for needles and pins. The rumpled sheets got covered in bits of cotton and thread, I sweated and drank pale tea with condensed milk, John fidgeted about the bed trying to find a comfortable position to write in.

A couple of hours later, the dress sewn on me, we climbed into a sailing boat with Ruta and Phyllis, about ten other guests and the crew, one of whom was called Luigi. After what seemed hours of cutting through a choppy evening sea with lava islands and crags, cliffs with tiny vineyards, passing Massine's island, the Isola de Galla, and on and on, we arrived in a cove, and wondered to each other whether the natives would be friendly. It was very beautiful, the small grey beach, the great crumbling house with its high double doors and ornate windows in which there was no glass. We crunched over the pebbles, Phyllis attenuated in lavender pants painted on like woad, the other women uncertain whether or not to wear their necklaces, fussing over their faces, shooting despairing *moues* at their lovers, all clutching reticules of some sort. Then the house. Whose house? Who was the host, the hostess? Cavernous rooms, completely bare, barns where paper fish dangled six-feet-long, two divans under a rush canopy, darkness and echo and fourteen people drifting about like ghosts.

Our hostess turned out to be a desperate Austrian, an antique dealer Ruta said, but he wouldn't lend her any money. This was a favourite remark of Ruta's, giving the impression of being surrounded by plaintive friends demanding the price of a pizza. After ten years of widowhood she had married a smooth English homosexual. She pressed whisky sours on us, poured out her life story, asked and would gratefully answer every intimate question, offered us a letter of introduction to the curator of Kenwood. Her shoulder straps slipped down, she grew older every minute, clutching the arm of a cold husband who shook her off impatiently. In the black nave of the barn was the impression, little more, of a fair girl in a black dress, Ophelia after drowning. She was the pupil, disciple and mistress of the old bearded painter and spoke a neat, shrill Kensington. She said that she couldn't paint Italy; that here she had taken to abstracts because there was nothing else to do. She thought it might be better in Wales. I sat on one of the divans with Countess Kayserling, a tall, gentle, youngish woman. She described her day in a low voice, with the inoffensive egoism of a child: they got up late, her husband worked, she did dressmaking, then a quarter of an hour's sunbathing on her terrace — too much sun made one *cretino* — lunch, siesta; around 3.30 a little swimming or a stroll, tea, in the evening a party, drinking of wine. In the autumn they sometimes walked in the gorges — I imagined them hand in hand like two primeval creatures, wandering between enormous rocks. In the winter she wore socks, two pullovers and sometimes a shawl tied round her head; it was frequently necessary to bathe the hands in warm water.

Later we all had dinner at the trattoria on the beach, a glittering patch of jabber in the enormous night.

'... Divine *shirt! But for me it must be lower — just*

59

that much lower!'

'I shall strip later and then you can slash it, darling. In any case I'm far too old for the shirt, I looked in the mirror and thought "I'm far too old..."'

'... Dear Geoffrey seems to live in a world of his own — I mean Transatlantic Lullaby and then silence — I have perfect pitch but I simply couldn't learn a tune of Geoffrey's. Ah, Cranks! I found that so moving, so true! ... Well, I was the Second Messenger in Richard III and Larry is marvellous, I mean he's dynamite. I have a small part in The Sleeping Prince — Larry says he simply won't make a film unless I'm in it. "I must have Bobby!"' he says ...'

'... Oh yes, we have a charming house, two bathrooms, one of them works — oh, several rooms. I sleep in the dining room on a small bed. In fact that might describe my whole life, a small bed in the dining room ...'

I wandered away and threw pebbles into the invisible sea until they all came crashing over the pebbles and we started for home. On the boat John and I huddled together. The engine began to stall. About a mile off shore it gave out completely and we rocked on a silent sea. Nobody did anything. The lights of Positano might have been Africa. At last the crew who wasn't Luigi got into a small dinghy, the sail was hoisted in the windless air and we were towed inch by inch towards the shore. Rugs were produced and fireworks began exploding from the mainland, bangs reverberated between the mountains, peacocks' tails of light spread and fell.

The next morning at 8.30 we were in a car going to Paestum: pink Greek temples burnt for centuries under the grill of sky, waste burned fields where lizards darted through tufts of grey tough grass, wind blowing perpetually across the plain. Julia jumped over ruins — 'Well, this is a very interesting little place!' The wind blew through pillars and four black priests with brief cases hurried, heads bent, across the sun. Heavens, how beautiful. At the Cinema Poseidon across the road, Rock Hudson.

Madelon and Julia were ill and put to bed. Painfully, moving like two dysentery-ridden refugees, John and I crept round to Casa Carolla to enquire, humbly, whether the Rich Americans might have Helga and Jeremy for an hour on their enormous terrace, perhaps even a go on the swing? This made a very awkward situation. The Rich Americans were fanatically conscious of what they called, with dread and respect, microbes. I had noticed a distasteful interest in the children's illness and Mom looking fearfully at a newly scratched mosquito bite on my arm. Sophe, their awful child, had visited us and probably carried home tales of doors open on tumbled beds, half naked children groaning among the lizards and verminous cats. Pop lumbered off to consult Mom; Mom appeared and said she must ask Shirl, but that Shirl and her Nanny — a peasant girl from the deep south of Italy — had a real horror of microbes and if the baby caught it well, she might give it to Sophe and Sophe might give it to them and they might give it to the Old Lady, whoever she might be, in which case they would never forgive themselves.

Naturally, we said stiffly, don't give it a thought. Goodbye. But now remorse, homeliness, got the better of them. They must do *something*, and of course the answer was pills. They gave pills, calculating the weight of each child and deducing the number of pills it should have. With a final, desperate bonhomie (but nothing could really make it any better) they invited us to a cocktail party. We tottered home, clutching the pills, to find Sally had joined the fever ward. Pills distributed, I lay on the bed while Deborah tied bits of bougainvillaea to toothpicks and John draped himself in my beads or fingered them nervously while he wrote at the desk and the sheets got covered in ash. The next day, after a perilous journey from Pompeii, we arrived back to find Daniel George saying of *The Bright Prison* that I was one of the very few living novelists who .. What fun, Caroline said, if we'd all been killed on the way back. Sucks to Daniel George, she said.

We went to Naples for the last time. Everywhere was the dry, sweet smell, sticking to the roof of one's mouth, of what I thought were bones. In the Cathedral, where the body of S. Gennaro is in one place, his blood in another, it was particularly strong. An old woman was carrying on a soundless argument with God, she gesticulated, shook her head, implored, threatened and finally, when some rapprochement had been reached, crossed herself, climbed to her feet and blew a delicate, cheeky kiss from the tips of two fingers towards the blazing altar.

Jumping and hopping on white-hot charcoal, we went to the Aquarium. Like Pompeii, the museums, the churches and cathedrals, it had a strong sense of something nasty, more sordid and at the same time more lifelike than mere fish or stones or saints. In the large, misty green tanks fish from the beginning of time flew and walked but seldom swam, looking like birds or flowers or mythical monsters but hardly ever like fish.

The octopus panted, its terrible membrane of a body like a squashed owl; a ridiculous field of pantomime marigolds was alive, breathing and strutting on tiny legs. The whole place, liquid and living as it was, stank of bones.

In the last few days we discovered Praiano and Hermann Minner, a stocky, bow-legged Belgian painter of great charm. One morning while John was in Naples I visited an exquisite grandfather called Han Harloff and found Hermann slicing potatoes. I stayed all morning and Hermann drew me, making me look both hard and sad, which was perhaps right but he didn't like it.

Now we're 6500 feet over the Mediterranean. Tonight Jean-Marie will dance in the Bucca and the Deisses will shiver in their palace, Brigida and Carola and the girl with the mournful eyes will sit on the wall waiting for nothing to happen. Han will relax in the chair his wife doesn't like, the antiflogistin pad fixed warmly over his chest, and Hermann, back in Praiano, will — what? Paint, perhaps, glad to be back, prowling softly about his house on bare feet and short legs, the gold chain and the gold tooth glinting, talking Flemish or some terrible Parisian argot to himself. Already, as we fly over Elba, the whole thing is a dream, I keep nudging my mind to try and remember, but there's only an irrational sense of disturbance, something left unfinished...

John, having more agile powers of invention, finally wrote the greater part of *With Love and Lizards*. When it was published Marghanita Laski attacked us for heartless exploitation of the children. This offended Deborah so much that she wrote Miss Laski an abusive letter on lined paper.

The following summer I went back to Positano by

myself. I didn't admit that Hermann Minner had much to do with it — more, I thought, a vague, romantic longing for something lost in my life: spontaneity, sensuality, anticipation — youth, I suppose. John, though he may have suspected the reason, was perfectly agreeable. He said he was incapable of jealousy and on the rare occasions it came to the surface turned it into something bland and manageable, which in this instance I chose to believe.

I stayed most of the time with Peter Ruta, the rest with Hermann in Praiano. It was the first time I had been 'unfaithful' to John, but there was never a moment of serious infidelity. I wrote to him every day, saying how much I loved and missed him, that I was eating whole garlic bulbs like apples, listening to scandalous tales about our friends of the previous year, sleeping until noon, being painted as a huge sprawling nude, becoming used to fighting my way on to 'buses and hurtling along precipitous roads on the backs of Vespas, describing everything in minute detail, except the one thing I felt didn't concern him. I relished it all, even occasionally telling myself that this was how I should be living, but I longed to go home. Though far more powerful, it was the same feeling that had brought me back to Positano — a feeling of something waiting to be resolved, but just out of reach; something that contained the one satisfactory answer, if only it could be snatched out of the future and realised.

Exactly thirty years later I went to stay with Deborah and her family in a Welsh cottage they had rented for the holidays and came across the copy of *With Love and Lizards* I had given to my mother, inscribed by me, in a bookshelf in the bedroom. Paul must have inherited it with the rest of her books when she died; after his death my sister-in-law presumably sent the lot to a jumble sale, where the unknown owners of this cottage bought it. Deborah went her version of very pale, thinking it a visitation. She took it with her when we left and it became favourite reading for my grandchildren.

CHAPTER SIX

After a brief and ineffectual first marriage my brother Paul had fallen in love with Jay Black, a remarkably pretty woman with a talent for making pot-pourri and plucking geese. She was married at the time to a doctor, Stephen Black, and had a son and a daughter about Madelon's age. For some reason her divorce was highly dramatic and Dr Black was headlined in the pulp press as 'the Beast of Lower Beeding.' In spite of the fact that John was appearing for her, I never knew precisely what was so beastly about the man. Finally Paul married her and became a step-father. He would have no children of his own. I often wondered if this was some sort of protest.

My father was due for retirement. Somehow, probably with my mother's help, he collected enough capital to contribute to a house in North London. Paul, Jay and her daughter Trudi moved into the upstairs flat, my parents took over the ground floor and garden. While my mother resolutely carried on living a country life as far as she could — pursuing the milkman's horse with a dustpan to scrape up its precious shit, planting Fragrant Cloud and Grandpa Dickson, baking bread, stripping lavender — my father gradually collapsed, sitting all day at his Vicar's desk with nothing to do except smoke and surrender to cancer. They were only a mile or so away but I seldom went to see him and remember him visiting us only once — that is, I remember his dreadfully swollen ankles and Jeremy in a clip-on bow tie crawling round them. My mother came frequently on the 'bus, bringing her galoshes and secateurs.

The last time I saw him, probably at her request, he was in bed in his study, the curtains drawn but not blocking out daylight. A cigarette smouldered between his fingers, but he was barely conscious and didn't notice when I took it away. As though vaguely remembering, he groped for my hands, lifted them and held them over his eyes. I can still feel the discomfort of sitting in this awkward position, knowing that I mustn't move. After a while he fell asleep.

He died soon afterwards — the only reason I think it must have been 1956 is because of what happened later. I know John said I was making an undue fuss about it, but have no recollection of either making or feeling fuss. The cremation at Golders Green has become confused with later cremations — the sense of hurry, the moment of awe as the coffin slides off-stage, the uneasy feeling of having cheated or been cheated. I know he has an entry in the Book of Memory, for which my mother chose a quote from Browning: ' 'Tis not what man does that exalts him, but what man would do.' It would have been hard to find a more appropriate epitaph.

In the Spring of 1957 Rachel Mackenzie of *The New Yorker* wrote to me asking for 'a long memoir'. She expected, she said, that my memoirs would be exceptional. I worried about it, feeling as though I were about to take an exam knowing that I'd done no work and hadn't the faintest grasp of the subject. The answer came one day as I was standing in the queue at the local supermarket: for the first time in my life I would try to write about my father. It wasn't easy, but slowly, as I worked, it became exciting. Possibly for my own protection, though I wasn't conscious of needing protection, I found myself writing about him as though he had no connection with me and discovered to my astonishment that I felt pity for him, even love. *The New Yorker* paid $970 for the piece and put me under contract for six stories a year. Together with my skimpy income from journalism this gave me an illusion of wealth. In one of our increasingly desperate attempts to solve the problem of the holidays I contributed most of it to the rent and furnishing of the nursery wing of a Victorian mansion in Norfolk.

John's vacations not only co-incided with the children's school holidays but were often longer. Although there was Helga now, we no longer had Willersey: this meant that for a third of the year there were seven idle people of varying ages in the house, all needing attention, occupation and three meals a day. John could write his novels with Alma Cogan blaring and children littering the floor, stopping quite equably to make an omelette or play Beggar My Neighbour, but even if there had been time this was impossible for me.

Why this particular problem should have been any different in rented houses I'm not at all sure — something to do with a sense of freedom, lack of responsibility. The children were busy with the sea, exploring a new garden; they didn't have to be walked in the park or marched round museums. We could picnic, improvise, make do. My mother was delighted to get out of London and took over most of the chores. It was obviously easier, but still doesn't explain why as Jeremy grew older he rarely spent more than a week of his holidays at home, even at Christmas.

John and I were still engrossed in each other but his flirtations — infatuations, whatever they were — were becoming an almost constant part of my life. Though bucket-and-spade holidays in a sharp east wind were some of our happiest times, staying in England would later become intolerable — there was always some reason for him to nip off to London, returning with sour offerings of guilt and remorse. I welcomed his eagerness to go abroad, even if the children didn't. In the future we traipsed further and further away, the South of France, Austria, Italy, Morocco, Spain, Bermuda. The moment the 'plane took off or the ferry sailed I had the illusion of safety, thinking that for the next few weeks we could live free of the unknown, invisible 'someone' who haunted my life at home. I never explained this to anyone, least of all Jeremy.

CHAPTER SEVEN

‎*1*

December 8 1957: *How long since I wrote here? Not since July, Positano. It is Sunday evening. John is at the Dorchester meeting, I think, Sydney Box. What's changed? Jeremy goes in the mornings to nursery school, talks of Lucy and Richard. Julia left Ballard Point and goes to the Frances Holland in Baker Street. We have a cook, a Vicar's daughter, and Elli, who leaves in 12 days.*

Now, at 39, I have to find that it's difficult to live with people any more. I only want to work and at the same time, noiselessly, to live; and be, if it were possible, happy in living as well as in working. But I'm not generous enough to do both, want my cake and am hungry, but haven't the stomach for having and eating. I twist my hair again like a schoolgirl, go to sleep unhappy and wake radiant to the thought of a peaceful weekday. I long for it and can't bear it to end — which it does with the key in the lock, 'Hullo? What's the plan?' we must have people in or go out, my room invaded, all routed and nothing left in its place. Of course it isn't my room, and I am bitterly wrong.

I was not only functioning again, but obsessive. A steady stream of stories poured into *The New Yorker*, a steady stream of dollars poured back. There was no need to look for ideas. I mined my life for incidents with a beginning, a middle and an end, finding that even the dreariest days contained nuggets of irony, farce, unpredictable behaviour. None of the stories could accurately be described as fiction; the moment I fabricated or attempted to get away from direct experience *The New Yorker* regretfully turned it down.

My editor, Rachel Mackenzie, was a genius. Nobody had ever been able to teach me anything, but she taught me how to write. The process, conducted by cable and mail in those days, was often painful. A child fell down a cliff and broke its leg: how high was the cliff? should the leg be sprained rather than broken? did it fall on sand or rock? how old, exactly, was the child? These quibbles maddened me but taught me the value of accuracy, or at least of accurate thinking. Redundancies, colloquialisms, adjectives, superlatives were wiped out, often inspite of my bitter protests. 'But Penelope dear,' she would ask mildly, 'what does this mean?' Since she died I have fallen hopelessly short of her standards, but at least I have had the opportunity to pass them on to other people.

The *Sunday Times* asked me to review fiction. This was brave of them, for I had no idea how fiction should be reviewed and simply relied on arrogance. Sometimes it worked. 'Osbert and I are *enthralled* by Miss Penelope Mortimer,' Edith Sitwell wrote from Castello di Monte-gufoni, and Beverly Nichols, with whom I don't feel I would have had much in common, told me I deserved 'a few late chrysanthemums − no, a great many of them − for that sparkling piece on Dylan Thomas. I pray you may never cast your steely eyes on any work of mine!' People's expectations seemed as low as their standards. In fact I was cheeky, opinionated, and totally ignorant of the rules I was apparently breaking. I didn't have the *nous* to disguise my impatience with sloppy writing and silly stories, consequently hurt many authors and made permanent enemies. I'm still not ashamed to say it was fun. For a long time if some critic attacked me with a particularly choice piece of virulence I found myself thinking 'He must have been pleased with that' and felt a stab of envy.

John had published five novels during the twelve years we had been together, but although my score was only two I was now the better-known writer. However piqued he may have been by this he was always supportive, and generous with his praise. I relied on his admiration more than his judgement; if he said something was 'very good' I tore it up, anxious about the missing hyperbole. He did, however, stop writing novels. Moving to drama, an area where I couldn't compete, he discovered his own voice. *The Dock Brief*, his first radio play and winner of the Italia Prize, introduced a character, inspired by his father who, in slightly different guises, would serve him indefatigably for the rest of his career.

I suppose it might be said (and undoubtedly was) that I was inventing characters based on John. Certainly I used writing to get rid of my scorn for some aspects of men in general, but none of them had his positive qualities; none of them were talented, funny or had any charm, none of them were sexually attractive except to girls known in that innocent age as 'dollies'. Similarly, although what I wrote was always assumed to be autobiographical, I never once wrote about myself, or the self who was doing the writing. All my women protagonists were victims of their insensitive husbands; none of them did any work; they had children, but didn't get much enjoyment out of them; they had obscure, meaningful problems, but never about the gas bill or school fees; they weren't particularly bright or particularly good-looking or particularly anything. God knows who they were, but I knew them well.

2

The success of *The Dock Brief* was a turning point. John was approached by Hollywood and we began to be relatively wealthy. A few workmen and Terence Conran in overalls turned the nursery into a kitchen with pine beams and concealed lighting. Cooker and sink were on opposite sides of the room, but once photographers had arranged pots of ivy and *objets d'art* and set the table with an unlikely number of wine glasses, candles and napkins (which they had to supply) photographs of it in glossy magazines looked impressive. John and I now had our own cars and the dark red hall was a riot of Sanderson's ivy. Helga had been replaced by an unending succession of Portuguese, Spanish, Australian and German girls. I remember none of them well except Rosemary, who dyed her hair a remarkably dazzling yellow and was Jeremy's first passion. Some were mournful and wept into the soup, some sprightly and competent, one or two had hard hearts and unpleasant dispositions. I always dreaded their arrival and nearly always dreaded them leaving when their time was up.

In some ways that final year of the Fifties incorporated everything that had gone before. Deborah, delighted, and Sally, miserable, went off to boarding school where they wore grey flannel shorts and sang Hymns Ancient

& Modern. In the spring I became pregnant. Jeremy and I, both pleased, called the baby 'Snooks' and speculated about its nature. In July I had a miscarriage; the baby was dead anyway. When John came to fetch me from hospital he told me Caroline had left home to live with a young actor. In spite of Julia, Jeremy and, whoever the au pair was at the time, the house seemed empty. Madelon finished Cambridge at the end of the summer term and took over Caroline's room. She found a job as statistician for Rothman's cigarettes and hung all the face flannels on little plastic hooks in the bathroom, but we didn't get on. In August we rented a house in the South of France and Jeremy learned to swim at Eden Roc. I wrote a story called *The Skylight* about a small boy who climbed through a skylight in a French house and couldn't be reached by his mother, only realising long after that it was about the miscarriage.

John's career of solitary novelist, conscientious lawyer, was replaced by one consisting almost entirely of Sprat, compensation for all he had missed. This new life demanded and supplied a succession of accessible girlfriends – he would never have referred to them as lovers. He felt that our marriage would be perfectly satisfactory if I could understand this and give him my blessing, but I couldn't. Actual sexual infidelity was the least of it, provided I wasn't expected to sympathise, but I furiously resented hints and confessions, implausible excuses, furtive muttering on the 'phone, a flowering of Carnaby Street shirts and medallions. I despised him for needing my sympathy as much as for the minor and clumsily conducted affairs. Perhaps it was the same contempt I had felt for my father, more readily available than tolerance; anyway it was equally lethal. At the same time there was a new kind of loneliness, supportable only because I knew that in the intervals between affairs there would be a short time of hectic reconciliation; and always, through every activity except work, there was an undercurrent of apprehension and mourning.

My third novel, *Daddy's Gone A-Hunting*, came out in September 1958. 'A remarkable and deeply disturbing achievement ... Pellucid, poetic, tart and compassionate' they said, but I hardly noticed.

3

We spent the Easter holidays that year in a rambling Edwardian house on top of the cliffs at Lyme Regis; it was creaking centimetre by centimetre towards the edge and later, I think, fell into the sea. John, now frantically occupied in the vacations, came at the weekends. We had an au pair called Ria — the only thing I remember about her — and my mother came, so it was possible to work. I was writing an adaptation of my story *The Renegade* for television, reviewing for Tony Godwin's *Bookman* and — perhaps the least likely job I ever had — writing a weekly Agony column in the *Daily Mail*. This brought in stacks of letters, many of them unanswerable.

Dear Ann, [my name was Ann Temple, after a doyen of Agony Aunts]
I am 55 years old and as I am bald have worn a wig since the age of 30. I have recently met a gentleman who has proposed marriage. I had given up hope and would like to accept this offer,
Would you advise me to tell him about the wig before

or after marriage? It might come as a shock after, but I do not want to put him off as you will understand.

I am anxious about this matter so hoping to hear from you. Yours truly . . .

Wherever we were in the holidays, Siriol Hugh-Jones brought her daughter Emma to stay, though both of them were slightly uneasy away from SW3. Emma and Jeremy were almost the same age and for the past four years we had pushed their prams, then buggies, round various parks, chattered over and across them with cigarettes in our mouths and deadlines to meet. To Siriol, who had come to it fairly late, motherhood was an exquisite anxiety. She was obsessed by the mechanics of the thing — vitamins, diet, clothing. We could be floating fifty yards off some Mediterranean shore and in a sudden panic she would demand to know if Daniel Neal sold woollen leggings. This anxiety was painful to her, in a pleasurable sort of way, but as the victim of so much devoted worry and vigilance, Emma grew pastier and snottier and by the age of five looked and often behaved like a deprived orphan. I don't think she and Jeremy particularly liked each other, but at Lyme Regis he persuaded her to climb on roofs and up trees and not be unduly terrified of crabs. Many of the friends who sprawled round Siriol's sitting room in London had been her contemporaries at Oxford and she was at her best with them, once she had learned that their interest in babies was limited. I see her sitting on the floor, shoes off, within reach of a box of Players Medium Navy Cut, bird-bright, apparently inexhaustible, eager to know everything. She didn't confide in me much — I never knew why she separated from her husband Derek Hart for a while, or what she felt about him — but we had some sort of understanding based on more than the children and I valued it highly.

Tag-ends of memory last the longest: I can still feel the pleasure of taking Jeremy to his first movie — *Tom Thumb* with Jessie Mathews and Bernard Miles — and watching him caper delightedly home through the Borough Council gardens, of playing with him in the sun all afternoon, moving tiny knights about in a jungle of daisies and grass, of sitting with Siriol under the cedar tree, watching the ant people down below on the sea-front in ballooning navy suits and white cardigans, little boys picking their painful way barefoot to boarding house tea.

And there is one more image: my mother always came to stay in the holidays. She crept about trying to be invisible when John was there and disapproved of me working; otherwise the children gave her much pleasure and I believe she enjoyed it. One afternoon she took her forty winks on the lawn, lying tidily on her back, hands clasped over her cardigan. I happened to be walking by with my camera and something about the way she lay, the expression on her face, made me stop and take a picture. When it was developed I saw my mother dead. The face was ashen, the repose far deeper than sleep, the folded hands terminally peaceful. She died thirteen years later but I suspect my mourning began the day I saw that photograph.

CHAPTER EIGHT

Any sane woman on discovering she was pregnant for the eighth time would have been horrified and rushed for an abortion. In spite of the unease in our marriage, my powers of self-persuasion were miraculous. Jeremy was six, off to school every morning in a round pink cap like a blancmange, Julia sixteen, Deborah and Sally away for two thirds of the year. Caroline, now at RADA, had her own flat and Madelon was surviving in Rome. John's first full-length stage play, *The Wrong Side Of The Park* had been a success and he was enthusiastically adapting most of his radio plays for the theatre. We had bought a permanent house for the holidays, Southend Cottage, near the Mortimers on the Chilterns. There had just been poor notices for my collected *New Yorker* stories and I was never going to write another word. Besides, a baby would be comforting.

That was the only argument I didn't put to Dr Gill. He reminded me that I was forty-two and my last pregnancy had failed. I told him my mother was forty-two when she had me. He said nevertheless he strongly recommended abortion. I said I had no intention of having an abortion. He asked me what John thought and I had to admit that I didn't know, except that he seemed amenable to the idea. 'Well,' Dr Gill said grimly, 'I suggest you discuss it with him.'

Discussion between John and myself was something

we could very seldom have; our ideas of importance differed and neither of us could understand the other's language when we were being serious. So I was tentative in my approach, merely dropping an idle, 'You do want it, don't you?' His argument was astonishingly solemn, as though he had given much thought to the matter. He knew he had made me unhappy, that he had made a lot of mistakes, but our marriage was the only important thing in his life. The future he had planned when Jeremy was born was still there and he passionately wanted to share it with me. Another baby would make that difficult, if not impossible. However, if that's what I really wanted...

I was impressed not so much by what he said as by the fact that he had said it at all, moved by his unusually serious manner, his disappointment, his sincerity. If the alternative was a happy life with John there was no question which I would choose. I gave in, agreeing not only to abortion, but also to sterilisation. It was a permanent commitment to John's happiness. My own, I assumed, would follow.

It did. When the operation was over I felt relieved of far more than an unknown baby or subsequent babies – I had been given the gift of an unused life. I was deeply, radiantly thankful to John. He was in Los Angeles and we wrote fondly to each other every day, our letters full of promises and resolutions, planning the miraculous years ahead. My room was full of flowers from people I didn't know.

On my first night back at Harben Road the house was taken over by Caroline for her nineteenth birthday party. I lay in bed contentedly listening to the thud of Bill

Haley and his Comets; then, needing to pee, lowered myself to the floor, started to walk across the room, and coughed. The wound split like a zip fastener, pouring blood. After a moment's astonishment I staggered across the landing and woke my mother, bursting in on her like one of the nastier moments in Jacobean melodrama. She wrapped me in bath towels, hauled me back to bed and telephoned the surgeon. He arrived swiftly, handsome, urbane, charming. It was curiously intimate, just the three of us, all the lights on, blood all over the place, the party downstairs carrying on regardless. In the ambulance I kept making terrible jokes. The ambulance men raised their eyebrows at each other and smiled politely.

Instead of welcoming John to our new life I was still in the clinic, sewn up like a mailbag, when he returned. He was adequately attentive, but I could recognise his impatience and felt guilty. It was a bad time to discover that he was having an affair; worse when it turned out that he had been involved in it since the beginning of my pregnancy. In these ironic circumstances, unfortunately for my peace of mind and for the children, I felt tricked into permanent loss.

May 9 1961: *Being pregnant, aborted, sterilised, wounded — it's not surprising, I know, that nothing heals. 'Involutionary depression' I read, but don't know what it means. All I want is for it to be over. When John goes in his neat tie and suit to meet the people to whom he has to talk, I am actually physically afraid. Was a time when I could pull myself together, as they say. Not now. Two hours to get through. I shout first of all, because you can in an empty house; you can do anything. Then sit on the stairs, this you can also do.*

Then walk up and down stairs, into rooms, nothing there, out of them again. Finally lie down on the bed, try to make myself sleep, but after a bit I get up and begin to pretend, with that afternoon feeling, that we are now yawning, getting ready to go out to the movies maybe, where, the Curzon, vaguely talking about where, leaving the house behind. So make up my face, brush carefully my hair. But it's no use. Nearly 3, time to fetch Jeremy. And the bitter thought that with her there was wine for lunch and the afternoon planned. This is unworthy, indeed mad, and brings nothing but more unhappiness. I only write it to remember how I felt today, & put it away with other things best forgotten.

CHAPTER NINE

Southend Cottage was not a cottage, but the sort of country house that demands swizzle sticks in decorated tumblers, three cars in the garage, weekend guests in Barbours and Hermès headscarves. I never felt at ease there. We moved in shortly after I came out of the nursing home, and certainly this had something to do with it. The cobbled wound remained a suppurating mess for about two months. No one suggested antibiotics so I just mopped it up. When it finally healed I was left with a stomach which looked as though it had been chewed by wolves. I searched through the small-ads in *Vogue* and found a place in Chiltern Street where they said they could do something about it. The treatment went on in a basement where I lay on a couch attached to a greedy machine called a trajector, an unpleasant but not unenjoyable sensation which cost far more than I could afford and didn't make the slightest difference.

John was writing one of his elegant, light-hearted plays about his affair, though not about my involvement in it. He would recite the choicer passages to the producer over the 'phone and couldn't understand why I minded so much. His confused feelings were more than he could bear but I lumbered him with them; the sight of my sickness and wretchedness was intolerable. There were bitter quarrels, savage recriminations. His invective was more brutal than he intended – why didn't I just get out, go, I was useless to everyone, I was hideous, why didn't I *die*? In the notebook I said *I'm sorry for you, but I can't do anything and you must communicate it all to some very reliable person or God because otherwise you're going to explode, or kill me, or go mad, or something quite out of the character you present to everyone else.* But all I actually did was fling myself at him, try to hammer him into some kind of understanding. 'Why not go and have a nice hot bath?' he would suggest encouragingly as he left for London.

I suppose anyone walking over the Common on a summer Sunday afternoon and glancing over the hedge into Southend Cottage garden might have felt a pang of envy. They could spot famous actors playing tennis, actresses lolling in the sun, producers and directors sprawled behind newspapers, a dozen children running naked through the orchard. Laughter and shouting would have been pleasantly distant, the whole scene one of prosperous content. Those friendly, amiable people never knew, I hope, how angry and frightened I was, how contemptuous of their appreciation of John's hospitality, their eagerness to laugh at his often cruel stories.

To remind myself, perhaps find some reassurance, for the first time in years I went to the Law Courts, heels rapping down the green foggy corridors, remembering the way. Defended case of Evans, Court One. The usher asked, 'Did you give him kippers for breakfast?' I was startled. Breakfast? Give him? 'He's had four glasses of water.' I crept into a back seat with the odd sensation of seeing someone unawares – familiar back of the neck topped by yellowing wig, unfamiliar voice full of authority. John was appearing for Evans, the husband, a stocky, balding fellow. Mrs Evans was dark, spectacled, impassive. 'She fell out of love with him − physically, that is.' It seemed she was wrong not to fancy him, though I could see that he would become revolting. Evans got his divorce; the wife was told to pay fifty pounds against costs. John looked at his watch, bundled his papers together, said something which made Evans' solicitor laugh out loud and hurried away without noticing me.

The summer vacation began. There were days on end when he didn't go to London. One August evening I walked out of the cottage and drove to the empty house in Harben Road, turned on the immersion heater, made the bed, poured myself a brandy and wrote *One thing I know: I cannot stand up with an appealing grin and pretend I'm somebody else, with a smooth stomach and a sawdust head. I cannot hear once more how he loves or hates me, blames me. I will not be reduced to an uncreative cretin scribbling in notebooks. At last I realise that there's a point beyond which one cannot go.*

I slept well. But in the morning I knew that I had tied myself so inextricably to the bedrail that no amount of will power could make me walk away. I couldn't withstand the children's concern and bewilderment, John's panic and promises. Like my mother twenty years before, I gave up after three days.

Relentlessly, we all went to Elba, where the beds were twin, the flies devoured, the food was bad and the only comfort was to lie on a rubber mattress rocking, like some abandoned aviator, in the middle of the broiling

PM and Caroline at the Butts.

Right: Caroline on the ornamental mushroom.

Left: Chancellor Dimont and Madelon.

Above: Kenneth Harrison, taken in 1978.

Below: Left to right: Caroline, Julia, Madelon 1947.

Randall Swingler.

Below: Wedding day. PM and JM.

Deborah aged about eighteen months.

...urnt House Farm and 'Henry' the estate wagon.

Sally at Burnt House Farm.

Left to right: Jeremy, Sally, Deborah, Julia, PM, Caroline, Madelon;
'Prince', Caroline's adored and contentious peke, in the centre.

The Mortimers' Christmas card, 1956.

Apparently we all lived in a small tent. Julia is missing.
© Mark Gerson

Sally warily faces the camera on her eighth birthday, Julia pours the drinks, Jeremy looks wistful, PM eager to please, Deborah pleased.

Opposite page: PM as Young Novelist.

Right: 23 Harben Road. It's still there.

Below: PM as Youngish Novelist.

Below right: Ditto, with JM as Young Playwright.
© Mark Gerson

In the sitting room at Harben Road – JM, Sally, Julia, PM and
Jeremy. (John's present for *A Villa in Summer* on the
mantelpiece.)

JM and Jeremy.

PM and JM.

Above left: Siriol Hart (Hugh-Jones) and daughter Emma.

Above right: JM and PM.

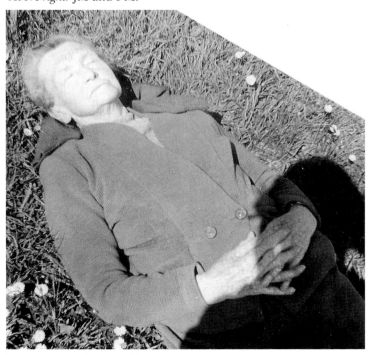

'I saw my mother dead.'

August on various beaches.

Derek Hart, PM, JM.

The Gondoly.

Jeremy and Deborah.

Jeremy vanquishes John.

At Southend Cottage.

Top left: Madelon.

Top right: Caroline 1957.

Above left: Julia 1962.

Above right: Jeremy and Deborah 1971.

Left: Sally 1969.

Jeremy, Deborah, PM, JM,
Mombassa 1968. We actually
caught them.

Right: With Derek Prouse and
lion cub, Cannes 1968.

Deborah's and Colin's wedding 1972. Humphrey and Pam Swingler, brother Paul (in hat), JM.

My mother with Ben, her first great-grandchild, 1973.

Above: SS Ackdeniz 1962.
P.M., Richard Kaufmann (at the end of the table), Caroline and Leslie Phillips on the right.

Above: Clive Donner.

Above right: David Mercer.

Below: Bette Davis, propounding.

Below right: PM and Jeremy, Easthampton NY.

The Old Post Office, Chastleton. PM and grand-daughter Jessica 1978.

PM and Jessica, Chastleton.

1978. Left to right: Jeremy, Sally, Deborah, Julia, Caroline, Madelon. PM on the floor.

sea. Our hotel was overlooked by a fortress prison for murderers with life sentences. Girls in bikinis displayed themselves on the rocks below, giggling at the frustrated howls coming through barred windows.

2

Back at the cottage, I seized on the Ban The Bomb rally of 17th September as a symbol of everything I was missing, telling myself that my life had been measured out in meals, vests, little Noddy, children-sized 'necessities', and that for once I wanted to join in, share something with my contemporaries. Nevertheless, I didn't go to Trafalgar Square that day. Why not? 'One cannot afford it,' John said, but that, whatever it meant, wouldn't have stopped me. Perhaps unconsciously I preferred to fume and fret in isolation rather than lose myself in a crowd. Whatever the reason, I went out and purposelessly dug the garden in the pouring rain, hurrying indoors to listen to news bulletins and watch television, pressing my nose to the world's window like some famished outcast. The next day Julia painted a CND slogan on the back of my car and other drivers waved cheerfully and pipped their horns. That was the nearest I ever came to being part of a Cause.

My television play *The Renegade*, written at Lyme Regis, was shown at last. The story concerned the night I ran away from school. Andrew Cruickshank misinterpreted my father and Jane Asher played me as a pretty, fragile teenager, far removed from the stocky, spectacled twelve-year-old I had actually been. John's parents came to supper and watched it appreciatively, Kathleen keeping up a *sotto voce* commentary. His agent, Margaret Ramsey, rang to say how much she had liked it. The notices were good.

... so it's been a difficult day, with 'I gave up writing novels', and tonight I spend alone, for which, if all were sensible, I should be thankful. If it weren't that I most horribly believe I shall never write again. The wind beats, rain pours, great insects bat their wings. Who to speak to, where to go? Eventually, after sounding tremendously cheery to the sparse characters who happen to be home, I talk to myself, though only in a whisper. I am on a peak, in a sea, and the sea is at storm. In a lighthouse I am. Oh lunacy. Here lie I. I could have been among the better writers. I could have lived a life. I could have gone up, not down. But I run about, round & round, run away from the pursuing heavy tread, the demand that like some machine drags the last bit of goodness out of impoverished soil. There's a great weight clamped over my writing hand. I don't know what I shall do.

I didn't know it then, but extreme despair is often the final stage of gestation. On Monday 6th November, the date I had married Charles almost a quarter of a century before, I was alone at the cottage. The Law term had started, the children were back at school. Thick fog blanketed the windows; no sound but an occasional groan from the radiators. I wandered round clearing up after the weekend, then sat down in front of the type-writer and idly, more for something to do than anything else, put in a sheet of paper. I stared at this for a while, then typed 'She went alone that autumn to the summit of a high, high hill' — a sentence which fortunately didn't survive, but lit up the dark corners of my heart.

November 25 1961: *Still calm and dry-eyed I write and write at my book. It's like being oiled, shining, on ball bearings once more. Whatever happens, the book is there. I love it, my graven image. For of course I have to feel guilty, even about this when at last it comes. I seem to be a thousand years old and yet ten at the same time. I want to sing very loudly and sweetly and love and love. In a moment of this I wrote 'Dear world' on the cover of my notebook. Dear world & life that lets me write and speak again.*

Very pretty, but John — who thinks it's marvellous, brilliant and so on — gets no benefit. What can I do? I write with a great effort at some kind of honesty and then feel a longing to hold his hand and say all's past, something's to come. So sometimes I even ring him up from my typewriter. But then, how cruel, everything dies except the writing.

3

The Pumpkin Eater was finished by the Spring. For months there had been a constant companion, often recalcitrant and maddening, sometimes boring, but occasionally coming up with great treats and staggering surprises. Now, except for the children, I was virtually alone again. Siriol, slowly dying of cancer and back with Derek, had withdrawn, as though needing to hide with her illness. I had come to have a paranoid distrust of other women, and most of them, I think, of me. There were flirtatious relationships with a few men — the vocabulary of sex is so limited that I can't think of a more accurate description. That these men were sexually attracted didn't necessarily mean they wanted to go to bed with me; that I was seldom sexually attracted to

87

them didn't alter the fact that I saw them as potential lovers. The wild inconsistency of this didn't escape me but made no difference. There was usually someone who could be 'phoned at two in the morning or summoned at short notice, someone to lunch with, take me to the movies, listen to my endless, repetitive *histoire*; and they put up with this because of the quality of my looks, not the quantity of my feelings. I gave them nothing, and felt very little for them.

With nowhere to put tenderness, admiration and respect I 'fell in love' like a schoolgirl, either with men whose talent far exceeded mine or men who were sufficiently mature, emotionally, to be friendly but sexually inaccessible. My sighs and yearnings must have been pleasurable up to a point; anyway they helped to fill the gap between the infatuated confidant of the moment and the obsessive struggle with John. My deep but over-cautious love for the children was something quite separate.

CHAPTER TEN

1

We spent that summer at the cottage. There were peas and marrows, raspberries and blackcurrants. My mother came to stay and placed sweet peas firmly in a fierce wire container. She also cut larkspurs, lilies, sweet williams and phlox so that instead of dying a natural death they dropped their shrivelled petals all over the furniture and expired nastily, hanging about until she buried them on the compost and ruthlessly amputated some more. She spent a lot of time reading to Jeremy, impersonating the voices of Mole and Thor, sinking to a whisper, rising to a lady-like roar, rallentando, crescendo, finale and the book closed until later. She then stood waiting for me to give her something to do, fingers steepled (because someone once told her it induced calm?). I heard her telling Jeremy that she would make the bags for the lavender he had stripped. I shouted, 'Don't make them! Just show him how!' and grieved her. Sometimes I caught her staring at me as though I were some unintelligible painting she was trying to understand.

We had an enormous PVC swimming pool which stood in a frame on the lawn; it was bright blue and quite hideous but the children enjoyed it except when it had to be cleaned out, which was fairly often. The slow afternoons went by to the accompaniment of splashing and shouting from one side of the garden, John and Deb playing tennis and shouting from the other.

'Love thirty!'

'It's not! It's thirty love!'

'Right, Debby — now I'll show you how you should be treated. Forty love!'

'Thirty fifteen!'

'Your ball was out!'

'It wasn't!'

'I saw it. Your ball was out.'

Jeremy was sitting in the canoe with Patsy, his constant companion. She was skinny and merry and a bit sly, wearing a shrunken cotton frock. The canoe, in fact, was on dry land. They rocked it idly, talking of this and that.

John said, 'Why don't you take them over, sweetie, and I can do some work.'

'I'm taking them for a great picnic tomorrow. They're quite happy here.'

'Why don't you take them for a great picnic today?'

'Because I'm taking them tomorrow.'

'You're a great help, I must say.'

I lay on my stomach in the orchard behind a plum tree. Dora, the Mortimers' cook, went home through the orchard, swearing at the birds for eating the cherries. Deborah walked remotely from the kitchen garden. I would have liked to talk to her but thought, 'leave her alone, don't swamp her.' She had been out on her bicycle and the beauty of the day would have filled her with yearning and hope and great clouds of music and worry about her figure. I roused myself and walked slowly towards the house. Sally came to show me a dress she had made for her doll; I said how smart it was and suggested she should dress all her dolls and send them to a children's home because bought dolls never have the right clothes and ... Pink-faced, giggling, chewing an apple, she actually hurried off to do this thing, or attempt it. Jeremy asked how to make pastry. I told him to ask my mother. Deborah had put some piece of mechanism in the fridge to contract. Remembering her look of exaltation, I suspected she would be difficult at supper.

Evening. The search for Elastoplast for someone's foot, for vests, for sandals, gathering discarded bits off the lawn, Jeremy and Patsy playing on the tennis court. 'Both of the dirty tennis balls are lucky,' Patsy said. 'Probably because they've had more experience,' Jeremy said. They seemed to move about aimlessly in the dusk, muttering together. Yet I knew they were never aimless.

When they were in bed I finished reading to them about Odysseus, who came home disguised as a beggar and made the plot with Telemachus and slaughtered the wooers, then stood in the firelight leaning against the mantelpiece while Penelope refused to believe who he was, because she'd been cheated so often; then he told her the secret of their bed, which nobody else knew, and she ran to him, but even then he warned her that he was off again. They heaved great sighs, but were disgusted by his cunning.

Odysseus and love for my son – scrubby hair, thoughtful, amused face, brain and heart both at work – altered the whole complexion of the evening. But the drab censor warned 'Don't let yourself love him too much or you'll become a devouring Mum and when there's an older Patsy you'll be hurt. Don't rely on him, or his love for you, or yours for him. Leave him alone.' So I left him, not independent or invulnerable, but alone. Of the curiously few regrets in my life, this is the greatest.

2

Madelon was living in Rome with various unsatisfactory lovers. Caroline had started a long affair with Leslie Phillips, a comedian of the 'Carry On' vintage with whom she was appearing in a West End play. Phillips was married, with four children; his attraction was puzzling, but she doted on him.

Julia had moved on to the French Lycée. The swaggering, nonchalant, eccentric child had become a secretive, troubled teenager, very beautiful, if spotty, with a boyfriend about whom I remember little except that he was interested in yachts. Kenneth was now Professor of Biochemistry at the University of Tehran. Until he left he used to come to see her regularly, arranging the date and exact time of his arrival at least a month in advance, arriving in his neat blue overcoat, bowler hat and spotted scarf with an assortment of very dull and enlightening books for the children. He would take Julia off to Madame Tussaud's or the National Gallery, which both of them seemed to enjoy, then doff his bowler and depart for Liverpool Street without a tremor of relief or regret. I couldn't believe that she missed him, but on the other hand I knew she was confused about the identity of her actual father and somehow knew it wasn't Charles. I wrote to Kenneth saying I thought she should be told and he nervously agreed to acknowledge her. Julia's casual comment — 'I always wondered why he gave me that bicycle' — was perhaps a cover-up for great emotion, but I suspect it just didn't seem particularly relevant to her life at the time. Three weeks later I put her on a 'plane for Tehran. On her return she talked of driving miles to see antiquities, but apparently their relationship had hardly been mentioned.

That August we took to the four younger ones to the Hotel Miramar in Malaga, a far cry from the cold, not too comfortable Spanish hotel of John's earlier fantasies. A week later a cable came demanding his immediate return. I knew Bill and Annie Davis, who lived not far away; he talked about Hemingway and she talked about friends who had energy and belonged to the international set, they had twelve Siamese cats and as many servants. The Davis's might have been helpful if they hadn't hated children, but only Julia, who didn't eat, drink, speak or do anything but look beautiful was admitted. There she met a rich young American, Ben Sonnenburg. Shortly before we were due to go home Sonnenburg approached me with great formality: Julia would stay behind with him in Spain. Would I kindly give him her passport. 'Certainly not,' I said, and many other things, only some of which were reasonable. Later I tackled Julia. She crouched in an armchair, curtained in hair, deaf to argument, appeal, and finally to orders. I don't know why I was so distraught, or quite what I wanted to protect her from, but she was only just seventeen and basically my values were staunchly middle-class. Desperate for some support — though god knows what I expected — I 'phoned John in London. He listened sympathetically then said it all sounded a great bore and where was the thermometer, he thought he might have a temperature. A few days later I gave Julia her passport and took the others home.

I can't say it was this that tipped the scales of my reason, but it is almost the last thing I remember for many weeks. I know that on our return we went to the cottage and that John was occupied putting on a play. One evening – perhaps Jeremy had already been put to bed – I drove to London. I let myself into the empty house and walked about, then fetched all the Soneril I had and swilled them down with a tumbler of neat brandy, believing this to be more lethal. The next thing I remember, two days later, was the New End Hospital and a nurse bending over me saying reprovingly, 'You are a silly girl, aren't you? What about all those lovely children?' They moved me to Greenways, the nursing home where Jeremy had been born, and gave me ECT, but I remember nothing. Julia, in Spain, was shown a newspaper cutting about my 'overdose', but no one in the family contacted her.

There is a blank until an afternoon in September. Caroline was visiting me. She said that she and Leslie Phillips had been asked by a Turkish shipping line to go on a publicity cruise to Istanbul and suggested that I went with them. We boarded the SS *Ackdeniz* at Marseilles. I was skeletally thin, still not entirely in my right mind. The other guests were journalists, minor actresses and the French film actor Jean Pierre Aumont. After a while I started having an affair with a German journalist, Richard Kaufmann. He was about my age, tall, shambling, pretty rather than handsome, reasonably intelligent.

There was a rumour, which both repelled and intrigued me, that he had been in the SS, though naturally he denied it.

Pumpkin Eater was published the week we docked at Genoa. I bought the *Express*, sat down on the stone steps and opened it to find the centre pages spread with a headline about the book and the news of my 'nervous breakdown'. I raced to the *gabinetto* and vomited again and again until I was hollow. To set against this, Caroline has a story of driving through Istanbul in a carriage while I sang 'I'm a genius! I'm a genius!' There is no reason why both shouldn't be true.

We were back in London on 5th October. My mother was in charge of Julia and seven-year-old Jeremy at Harben Road. I have no idea what happened that week apart from learning that John had a new romantic interest called Bobbie, and an overwhelming terror of his insistent presence and absence. On October 12th I drove to Switzerland, taking Caroline with me.

3

I suspect now that this was all an elaborate game, a variation on a theme that had become unbearably familiar. At the time I hoped, rather than believed, that it was real. Two days after we arrived I took Caroline to Zurich airport, drove back to Ascona and rented a flat over a baker's shop. My mother wrote with some relish that Julia had 'gone wild'. I rang John in the unrealistic hope that I could ask him to take care of her. 'Bobbie's going away this week,' he said. 'I'm perfectly free. Why don't I come over?'

Every day I would take my book to a restaurant overlooking the lake. The only other regular was a young man with a poodle; he was always writing letters and never looked up. I stayed there as long as possible, then walked back by way of the Post Office, dreading a letter from my mother, hoping for one from Caroline. I had received no further news of *Pumpkin Eater* and don't remember being particularly interested. One afternoon there was a cable:

DEAR PENELOPE AFTER MONTHS OF SOUL SEARCHING HAVE COME TO THE FOOLISH DECISION THAT I CAN MAKE AS GHASTLY A FILM OUT OF YOUR GHASTLY BOOK AS ANYONE ELSE STOP ... HOPE ALL IS WELL AND THAT YOU WILL NOT BE TOO MISERABLE AT THIS NEWS LOVE JACK CLAYTON

The old man in the Post Office didn't look as though he had received any good news since the invention of the cuckoo clock. I ran back to the flat and scribbled a note to the young man with the poodle. It turned out that he was a pianist and had just won some prestigious prize; that evening we drank a bottle of champagne and congratulated each other.

I had been longing for the children, but only as a ghost might long to return to life. Now I began to miss them urgently, with positive intention, appalled by the time wasted and the damage done. But still I couldn't make myself go back. I was frightened by the possibility that our marriage was over, terrified by the probability that it wasn't. John seemed to have no opinion either way. On 9th November he came for the weekend. 'Let's go to bed,' he said, 'and forget all this nonsense.'

96

Perhaps this was the way to deal with it; perhaps it was time I learned something from him, rather than always assuming I knew best. We parted on a note of mutual affection and respect. I returned home shortly afterwards.

4

The success of *The Pumpkin Eater* pleased me, though I couldn't understand it. The literary establishment, with its clubs and societies and guilds and conferences, wine and cheese, coffee and buns, was kindly. Lacking any urge to join in or get together or be organised I didn't understand what it was for, and I still don't. Perhaps I missed many golden opportunities — but to do, to be what? Nothing I wanted.

However, when my American publisher asked me to go to the States for a two-week publicity tour I agreed with enthusiasm, remembering that when Count Potocski had cast my horoscope it had predicted my fortune would be made on Broadway. My editor, a well-intentioned young man named Bob Gutwillig, met me at the airport and took me to the Fifth Avenue Hotel down by Washington Square. Since he lived just round the corner he said it would be convenient.

I don't know what the Fifth Avenue Hotel is like now, if it still exists, but in 1962 it seemed to be a sort of gaunt doss-house, hundreds of sparsely furnished rooms leading off miles of grimy corridor, no room service, no restaurant, as far as I could tell no people. New York sirened and flashed fifty floors down from my filthy, unopenable window. I sat on my bed most of the night, more frightened than I had ever been in my life.

Four days later — it was Caroline's twenty-first birthday — I checked out of the hotel at dawn and took my luggage to the air terminal. The London flight didn't leave until the evening. I spent the day walking up and down Avenues, in and out of department stores, carrying a gold basket full of hundreds of dollars and my return ticket home. When I thought about being home my eyes stung. I found myself outside Macy's, which at least I'd heard about, but was so alarmed by the miles of squalor that I walked straight through it and out into some long, anonymous street where everyone seemed violent and derelict, not black or white but the colour of dirty cardboard. I hurried up Seventh Avenue and back again, block after block, hideous, tatty clothes and greetings cards, Walk, Don't Walk, not daring to think about the consequences of running away, in terms of my own unreliability; not knowing where to stop or daring to stop. Into a great card shop like a nightmare, aisle after aisle of paper doyleys and bridge scores; out again, buying nothing, nothing to buy; walking uptown with the possibility that I should be walking down. 'You're a lonesome girl,' one of the cab drivers said. He pointed out a great dirty hotel like St Pancras, 'That's where the wrestlers hang out'; lying on the roof with their long yellow and orange hair.

By four o'clock, back and legs aching, face frozen, I stopped in one of the Schraffts on Fifth Avenue: middle-aged women in hats drinking tea, middle-aged waitresses, chandeliers, Easter bunnies, CANDY BY MAIL ANY-WHERE. The matrons stared at me. I couldn't bear being looked at, so although there was still another three hours until the releasing 'bus to the airport I moved on. Two hours later I sat in the furthest corner of the bar at the air terminal drinking brandy and soda. All I dared think about was getting home, being at home. Even more frightened by myself than by New York, I swore I would never, never complain or try to break free again, but thank god and keep quiet and finally die in my bed.

Bob Gutwillig sat down, saying 'I thought you'd be here.' There were no questions or recriminations. He took my hand as though I were having a tooth pulled without anaesthetic. Then he drove me to the airport. Before I left to go through Departures he gave me a farewell kiss. 'What will become of you?' he asked.

CHAPTER ELEVEN

None of my past clumsy attempts to assert myself — I suppose that's what they were — alarmed me as much as this. I was forty-four-years-old and had felt like a five-year-old, totally incapable of dealing with adult demands, nothing but a howling need to be taken home and protected from the unmanageable grown-up world. Or so I say now. At the time, I only felt in urgent need of help and advice.

Dr Wollf was a wizened, amused, wise little man. For the first few sessions he listened patiently, though with an abstracted expression, to confused descriptions of my marriage, six children, their four fathers, my writing, the abortion, the pills, the ECT, the flight to Ascona, the bolt from New York. Then one day he said gently, 'Yes, Mrs Mortimer ... Should we perhaps begin?' Begin? So I went through it all again, in case he hadn't understood: the bolt from New York, the flight to Ascona, the ECT, the pills, the abortion, the writing, the children, the marriage. He sighed, glancing at the ormolu clock on the mantelpiece.

I became fond of Dr Wollf and was faithful to him until evil influences lured me away. Even so the memory I connect most clearly with him concerns the magazines in his waiting room — no last year's *Country Life* or ancient *Tatler*, but stacks of Elizabeth Taylor skittish in the bath, the 1001 nights of Frank Sinatra, Moody Moments with Marilyn. For some unfathomable reason I felt they were unworthy of Dr Wollf and told him so. The next time I went they had gone. Probably it was a coincidence and they would have been thrown out anyway, but I watched a young man disconsolately reading the small print at the back of the *Evening Standard* and felt horribly guilty. *A dreadful puritan Harold Wilsonish Victoriana, that's what I stand for. Why don't I keep my mouth shut and stop agitating for the right things for the wrong reasons? Or is it the other way round?* I put this to Dr Wollf and he smiled enigmatically.

2

Jack Clayton was one of the very few visitors to the cottage I felt at ease with and liked. When he was thinking of screenwriters for *The Pumpkin Eater* he summoned me for a formal interview. What, he asked gravely, would I say the story was about? My mind went blank for what seemed some minutes, then I said 'Money.' He raised his eyebrows a fraction and scribbled something down. The job was offered to Harold Pinter.

We had known Harold since *A Slight Ache* was produced at the Arts Theatre with John's *Lunch Hour* and N. F. Simpson's *The Form*. At that time they were all lumped together as *nouvelle vague* playwrights, but since then John had eased towards Shaftesbury Avenue and Harold soared to solitary eminence with *The Caretaker*. I loved and admired him, for me a unique combination. If

Pumpkin Eater had still been mine to give, I would have given it to him with all my heart.

Jack had his own interpretation of the story — I never knew exactly what it was, but it was this he wanted to film and presumably instructed Harold to write. The only thing I was asked to do was appear for publicity pictures with James Mason, who was playing my most detested character, and I was kept at arm's length during the shooting; I accepted this with an ill grace, though occasionally had surreptitious meetings with Harold. Apart from one ghoulish scene in a hairdresser's, which was vintage Pinter, he stayed meticulously faithful to the dialogue. The characters and their behaviour were, to me, almost unrecognisable.

The surface story of *Pumpkin Eater* is written here. The underlying story of childhood, which I thought essential, was intended to illustrate that those who cannot remember experience are condemned to repeat it. Years later I would write a more adventurous novel on this theme, but at the time of *Pumpkin Eater* it was just a simple assumption that you can't have an effect without a cause. All this was considered unnecessary to the movie. The fantasy hoards of children were reduced to three plain, correctly dressed, well-mannered poppets and a mute toddler; the protagonist was given a name, couturier clothes and artistic lighting. Since she was the beautiful Anne Bancroft, married to the thoroughly decent, pipe-smoking Peter Finch I, for one, couldn't see what she had to complain about.

My main criticism, which I passionately expressed to Harold, was of the *dénouement*. In the novel the woman does a bolt to her 'high hill' (a tower, for some Freudian reason) and is tracked down and captured by her innumerable children; her husband, Jake, knowing that this is the only strategy that will succeed, delays his appearance until the capture is over. In the movie courageous Finch strides over the horizon with the mingy family tagging along behind. At first sight of him Bancroft capitulates and accepts a loving cup or can of Worthington.

> *Jake offers a can of beer to Jo.*
> JAKE: Want one?
> JO: Yes, I'll have one.
> *She takes it and starts drinking from the can.*
> FADE OUT

Harold sent me a copy of the script with 'I'm sorry' scrawled across the title page. However, I admit that the picture had style and may have said something to the English middle classes about their condition, if not about human nature. It can still sometimes be found at unlikely hours on tv, comfortably sandwiched between commercials.

3

During the first fourteen years of our marriage I had seldom been actually 'unfaithful', and then only when I was far away. None of these scanty affairs made much impression, though those with Richard and Hermann at least benefited from a degree of fantasy. Now, out of competitiveness as much as loneliness, I abandoned my prim objections to loveless sex for the second time, and took it when it offered.

Jeffrey Knight was an academic, unlikely among our theatre and film acquaintances. I couldn't have been attracted to him because of his personal charm, for he didn't have any; I can only think it was his formidable intelligence and the fact that he fell heavily in love with me. For some bewildering reason John invited him to the cottage for the weekend. I think Jeffrey and I must have been to bed together by then, but the event or events were so unmemorable that I can't be sure. We sat in a field among cows. 'I'm so furious!' he exclaimed, punching his unpleasant knees in emphasis. 'I want to get you somewhere where I could talk to you for a week without stopping!' Then he made a vehement speech about it being impossible for me to go on living with John, a man out of touch with reality, a man with no recognition. 'I don't like him' he finished flatly, as though that settled it. In a way I was reluctant to listen. In a way it was a relief. I was so enclosed and isolated that I often wondered how much was real, how much imagined. For someone from the outside to confirm even a fraction of my feelings at least meant I wasn't crazy. I just wished it hadn't been Jeffrey.

That September John and I flew to Edinburgh for the Festival. To wile away boring journeys we were in the habit of scribbling notes to each other, usually in some sort of rhyme:

PM: It's all very well for A. Wesker, W. Mankowitz,
   J. Mortimer, T. Allen,
   D. Tutin & J. Plowright on this flight
   Which gives me such a fright
   But I'm not sure that I wouldn't be more right on
   The diesel to Brighton.
JM: You are completely real BEAUT
   iful in your golden suit

And none here, definitely including Miss Tute,
Is a novelist of International REPUTE
So why not RELAX?

I had nothing to sell, no position to maintain or struggle for, it was a relief to be among talented people who didn't think of me as mother-of-six or author of *Pumpkin Eater*. I relaxed rather more than John, avoiding most of the parties and spending many evenings listening and talking like a relapsed Trappist in shabby bed-sitting rooms. I don't remember in which of these I met David Mercer. I had vaguely heard of him as a drunken Yorkshireman who wrote extraordinary plays for television.

Mercer and I appeared to be poles apart, but we had much in common. His childhood was spent in Wakefield among pits and factories and brass bands, mine in a country Vicarage, but we both thought of our early years as a time of sun and safety and were unable to reconcile ourselves to the adult lives we had chosen, or stumbled into. In our different ways we were both exiles mourning for Eden and we both reacted to this affliction with a sort of glum hilarity. We were also stern puritans at heart, guiltily aware of compromising our ideals; Mercer's were lofty and political and mine (if they could be defined at all) limited and personal, but the need, if not its expression, was the same. God knows he wasn't an easy man, a chip on his shoulder the size of a blunderbuss, tedious and unmanageable when drunk, often untrustworthy, sometimes an out-and-out coward. All I can say is that he was truly lovable. The relationship that started in Edinburgh changed a great deal over the next fifteen years, but my affection for him never altered.

Madelon was home when we returned from Edinburgh. One evening when John was out, Mercer, clasping bottles of wine, expansively drunk, stumbled in with a romantic-looking friend in dark glasses and a trench coat, introduced as the Polish actor Zbigniew Cybulski, star of Wajda's *Ashes and Diamonds*. We decided that we should call on Caroline to share whatever it was we were celebrating. It must have been past midnight when we got there. We were probably making quite a bit of noise; anyway she appeared at the window before we rang the bell and didn't hurry to let us in. We were unaware that the unfortunate Leslie Phillips, realising that he was about to be discovered, had clambered out of a back window and was now clinging perilously to the ledge.

Mercer made himself comfortable, Cybulski gazed admiringly at Caroline through his shades, Caroline nervously offered coffee, we chatted leisurely about this and that. Cybulski edged nearer to Caroline; he may even have taken her hand. Suddenly the curtains billowed open and Phillips, very cold and angry, fell into the room. It was a great entrance. Cybulski, shocked out of his few words of English, implored Mercer to translate to Caroline, 'It wasn't my idea to come and I'm sorry to disturb you, but I stayed because of your beautiful eyes.' This didn't help. For some reason Phillips attacked the gas fire, which satisfactorily broke. Madelon raced into the kitchen and started breaking china. Mercer said, 'Well, I must be off' and vanished. Cybulski followed me home, shaking his head and muttering reproaches to himself. I went to bed, leaving him sitting morosely at the kitchen table.

The next morning all that seemed to be left of Cybulski was a pair of dark glasses on the draining board. Mercer was anxious, so I asked Jeremy to look round the house and see if he could find a Polish actor. He came back saying there was someone in Madelon's room, he might be a Polish actor. I went up to find Cybulski kneeling on the floor, propped by a chair and fast asleep, spotlit by a shaft of sunlight.

Mercer was tumultuously in love. At one time or another he was tumultuously in love with practically every woman he ever knew, so for him it was hardly a new experience. For me, however, it was. Here was a man I could love, even if I wasn't convincingly 'in' love; a man I warmed to, admired, understood. He made absolutely no attempt to disguise his passion, declaring it in the butcher's while I was buying twelve lamb chops, to the children, to John, to the world at large; presumably to his wife, whom I very seldom saw.

The problem, as usual, was myself. It was now that I first realised that even while making love there was a voice warning *noli me tangere*. I was a vigorous, normal woman, not a helpless mouse in a laboratory, but it was as though all my sexual impulses had been conditioned to respond to one particular stimulus and that, for better (he was my husband) or worse (he was an unsatisfactory husband), was John. I longed for something, someone, to rid me of this disability. A number of men would try, and as many psychiatrists; I myself tried desperately, with little success. Perhaps a woman might have been the answer, but I was far too timid to venture into a different world and violently rejected any invitation to do so. There it was. I flamed, I flickered enticingly, I cast an alluring light promising welcome; but when the lovers swooped in out of the dark all they found was a charred match and a note saying Gone Away.

CHAPTER TWELVE

1

Mercer wrote his first, rather bitter stage play, *Ride A Cock-Horse* in 1964 and I went to New York to work for Otto Preminger and money. The story I was meant to be scripting was *Bunny Lake is Missing*, a rather ordinary tale about a child who vanished and turned out to have been kidnapped by its grandmother. This seemed too predictable. I pondered it and invented a psychopath, an incestuous brother insanely jealous of his sister's child. Most of the action was set in Jeremy's nursery school, much to the gratification of the ladies who ran it and the fury of the mothers who had to keep their darlings at home while it was being shot.

That, however, was some way off. Again I found myself in a vast, hostile hotel in New York, but this time provided with a typewriter. Otto Preminger, belying his reputation, was charming, friendly and sympathetic, conducting me round his formidable art collection, feeding and champagning me, pointing out the spotlit Henry Moore in his garden which he had placed on a turntable for the benefit of Tennessee Williams over the way. But I knew no one else, and had far too little confidence to call the few introductions I had been given. Myself, the typewriter and room service were a depressing combination. I walked through the Columbia offices one day straight into Otto's sanctum. 'I want to go home,' I said. 'Naturally, darlink,' he said, and told some underling to fix my flight. 'You miss your children,' he said, 'That is at it should be.' It was one of the rare occasions when I saw that there was an advantage in being a woman.

But even when I was back at my familiar desk I couldn't write it. I have always been paralysed when confronting fiction. Who are these people? What makes them behave as they do? How do they talk, brush their teeth? What do they remember? Plots are consequences of behaviour and I have no idea how to impose one on a set of characters I don't know. John, on the other hand, could do it with ease. Otto amiably agreed to my suggestion that we should collaborate and summoned us to Hawaii, where he was shooting the bombing of Pearl Harbour for *In Harm's Way*. We hung about for three days, cowering under explosions that shook the hotel and smothered the palm trees in dust; then, during a brief truce, Preminger and John discussed the dramatic possibilities of losing a five-year-old in Hampstead. The whole thing had become so unreal that I went to sleep with my eyes open, waking with a start to murmur what I hoped were appropriate comments.

On our return John wrote the script in a fortnight. I haven't read it since, and have no idea how much I contributed beyond the basic story – certainly Laurence Olivier's Chief Inspector and Noël Coward's sinister homosexual were entirely John's. *Bunny Lake* appears as a stop-gap on television more frequently than *Pumpkin Eater*. I imagine its archaic black and white images watched by haggard insomniacs in dressing gowns flickering unheeded in dark bedrooms. Preminger was rather proud of it.

When I was working well — which at the moment I wasn't — I was so cocooned that little else seemed to matter. Now, though I no longer thought of being dead or driving vast distances, it had become essential to detach myself in some way from John's life. I couldn't get away from the black, puckered, vertical scar that started at my navel, but the messages he seemed deliberately to put in my way stated quite clearly to me that I was sterile, that however hard I tried the creative, dangerous side of sex was impossible for me. I had to find a bolt hole, a place where I imagined I could 'be myself'. I couldn't and didn't face up to the fact that this implied separation from the children.

I took a painter's studio that almost literally hung over the mainline railway track between South Hampstead and Kilburn High Road stations. On the rare occasions when I stayed the night it was like sleeping in a pulverizer. The studio was a recent conversion, rather chic, with an open stairway leading to a platform bedroom built in ubiquitous pine, a bathroom and a galley kitchen. I went there sometimes after supper or on my way home from an evening out to scribble on its discreetly headed writing paper. It cost me five pounds a week. John was uneasy about it at first, but once he realised that its main purpose was for holding children's parties he more or less forgot its existence. Two years later I sublet it to the young man from Ascona, though without his poodle. He installed a Steinway and must have played everything *fortissimo* to compete with the trains. Shortly after he moved out he hanged himself. His name was Stephen.

The studio was an unrealised fantasy, but it wasn't altogether a failure. I began to see that some sort of separation might be possible if I had somewhere that could house the children. I knew it was up to me. I was the one who insisted on going where the sign said NO TRESPASSERS, took hazardous short-cuts, crawled through barbed wire. John waited for disaster to occur and then stepped out of it, a little ruffled perhaps, but virtually undamaged.

The original lease on Harben Road had been extended twice; its future, like ours, was uncertain. The Eyre Estate said they were going to pull it down, but were unable to tell us when. We stopped bothering to repair it; the walls slowly cracked, the ivy wilted. If we were going to stay together (the alternative was still unrecognised, a sharp pain in the night, a momentary giddiness) we should look for another house which would at least see us through until Jeremy left school. Although we had no capital and insufficient faith we spent many evenings driving round St John's Wood and Hampstead weighing up the pros and cons of terraced splendour in Regent's Park and Georgian cottages overlooking the Heath. Did either of us really believe in it? Belief in the future came and went as regularly as the tide.

But its volume was diminishing, and by the beginning of the following year had dried up altogether. In one of his fevered and probably justified panics about money, John sold the cottage. I had never felt warmly towards it, except through the children, but now we were trapped. In January I took a flat in Aberdare Gardens, round a few corners from Harben Road.

John, not taking this latest move seriously, said we

must stay together because of Jeremy. Jeremy was nine years old and, with all his sisters away, virtually an only child. My feeling, too full of regret and guilt to be a specific memory, is that apart from school he spent much of his time with the current 'help', a plump, elderly Mrs Webber who suffered from cystitis, and the television. Was this the kind of life he would lead for the rest of his schooldays, used as our only source of happiness, stifled by our problems, never knowing from one week to the next what was going to happen? A different sort of child might have survived it − plenty of them do − but I could already see him becoming more withdrawn and fearful, his baby jauntiness grown shadowy, even his physical presence becoming shadowy, as though by a great effort of will he was trying to become invisible. When I tried to say all this, John was exasperated: 'Why don't you do something about it then?' Under the circumstances I could only think of one practical thing to do, and that was to send him away.

It was unthinkable that he should live without women. In those days the few co-educational boarding schools there were seemed to cater mainly for wealthy delinquents; only Bedales, in spite of its homespun Fabian traditions and tendency to sandals, sounded possible. I wrote to Dunhurst, its junior school, asking if they would have a place for Jeremy in September. Not a chance, the headmaster replied, though rather more elegantly. I wrote again, insisting that he should at least see me. After we had talked for some time he said oh well, it might mean his own son sleeping in the bath, but all right. I was taken round the school by an intellectual, sombre lad whose ambition was to be an economist.

Wherever I looked, from the dormitories to the library to the bunsen burners to the games fields, I asked myself 'Jeremy?' and couldn't imagine him. But I couldn't imagine him sitting in front of the television with Mrs Webber either. Bleak, sober, responsible, I stayed the night in a dun and crimson coloured hotel on the Hog's Back and went home to report to John. The flat wouldn't be available until September. I decided to move in on 22nd September, the day after Jeremy was due to go to Dunhurst.

A week later my diary baldly states 'Rome to see Visconti re Tarnowska.' I stare at it, worry it like a piece of rag, turn it over and over, but nothing is revealed except a large man sitting in a garden saying 'I thought you would wear a hat with cherries on it'; the amphitheatre at Spoleto, interminable *Elijah* filling the sky, Visconti's entourage, a row of pale, handsome profiles, either side of us; a grey Picasso jug, of which I had a copy, standing on a corner table. The project was a film for Romy Schneider, based on the scandalous life of a Countess Tarnowska. I suppose we discussed it, though since Visconti's English was negligible and my Italian consisted of a phrase I had learned by heart in Ascona – 'Io vado a Milano per incontrare mia figlia si chiama Julia' – I can't think we got very far. One of his associates, a sympathetic and troubled man called Gene Lerner, lived in Belgravia and would keep an encouraging eye on me. Having reassured Visconti that I didn't wear a hat with cherries on it I went away with the formidable prospect of writing a script worthy of him.

It was now August, but as though it were the last weeks of a terminal illness or an imminent execution the future was seldom mentioned and never discussed. We migrated as usual, this time to a house in Mijas, a village perched on the mountains behind Torremolinos — ourselves, the three younger children, the essential Patsy, three teenaged friends of Deborah's and a tutor called Rohun, meant to prepare Jeremy for the academic rigours ahead. Kenneth and Kathleen Tynan were staying nearby. Although they were quarrelling bitterly at the time there were a few evenings of frantic Sprat, which John enjoyed. After they left, since there were two giggling girls from the village to do the cooking and housework, I set up my typewriter in the dark cave of the living room, well away from the grilling sun and the bedlam of the swimming pool and confronted Countess Tarnowska. Images filled my head, streamed on to paper; soon I was working twelve hours a day. Gene Lerner, wearing a turquoise playsuit and a yachting cap, was staying in Torremolinos. I delivered sections of the script to him as they were done, then pounded on, stopping reluctantly for meals, refusing to be put off by John's frustration and boredom.

It wasn't easy, particularly at night after Jeremy and Patsy were in bed. The teenagers, reluctantly taking Rohun, would set off on their own mysterious pursuits. John seemed obsessed by food, possibly because I wasn't providing it, and would insist on trying to discuss tomorrow's lunch. The years and years of oranges, apples, butter, cheese, tea, Nescafé, bread, chocolate biscuits would be touched on until I escaped outside into the blazing moonlight. The sun doesn't bathe, fill like the moon; there might be the sound of a distant mouth organ, while back in the living room my desperate husband grumbled on about sausages, bacon, Ajax. I had the curious, not altogether unpleasant sensation that my heart was stretching, expanding, attenuating until it became an open palm. If we could have shared our unhappiness instead of using it as a weapon there might have been some hope. I doubt whether it occurred to either of us that this was possible.

I had decided to spend my *Pumpkin Eater* money on some sort of house, shack, *pied à terre* near Bedales and asked Kathy Tynan to investigate. She found one with the promising name of Stable Cottage. I flew back to England to see it and found a red-brick semi in a newish middle-class housing estate about quarter of a mile from the school. It had nothing to recommend it beyond six reasonably sized rooms and a strip of garden, but I bought it nevertheless, hoping that it would make the parting with Jeremy less final. While I was in London I met Dr Barrington Cooper for the first time and try to remember what he looked like, since he plays a large part in this story: fairly small, portly, an astrakhan collar to his overcoat and a prosperous air, his voice soothing and low, a desirable thing in doctors, with an almost too perfect Oxbridge enunciation. I returned to Mijas and Countess Tarnowska and didn't see him again for a year.

By the time we got back to Harben Road the future was in front of us like a wall that had to be scaled. Beating one's head against it hurts the head, not the wall; weeping and wailing in its shadow only makes it seem higher, more unscaleable. The flat in Aberdare Gardens was empty. I moved in furniture, fixed the fridge, made the bed. John said I should be home in three weeks; Al Alvarez, whose constant gloom was comforting at that time, bet me five shillings I wouldn't last two days. Nobody believed in it, least of all myself.

I bought Jeremy's uniform, sewed on name tapes, packed his new trunk. He was full of chat and puns, whistling about the place. I longed to cry in private in the arms of someone who was also sad, also trying to be tough about it. Perhaps I should have recognised that person in John, but now the distant prospect was a reality he seemed bewildered. He could explain very clearly his need to live and work alone, his reluctance to perform the role of 'father' and 'husband', but at the same time he demanded why did it have to happen, this torture? Why couldn't we stop all this nonsense about separating, sending Jeremy away? Why couldn't I care for them, prop both of them up, allow him his longed-for freedom? Because in order to do that I would have to become somebody I might prefer, but could never be.

Julia had gone to live with the yacht enthusiast in a Knightsbridge basement; Deborah and Sally went back to school.

21 September 1965: *We took Jeremy in his great new suit ... At Dunhurst it was rather disorganised, the headmaster brisk, no one to leave him with. Jeremy said matter of factly 'I don't want to stay here' and complained in an uncomplaining voice that we were just 'dumping' him. I asked if there was someone to leave him with and they found a spectacled quiet child called Clement Edwards. Jeremy said 'Well ... g'bye' and went off with Edwards and the others. Last seen he was walking across the lawn with them and the tea bell was ringing.*

John said 'Now you can cry', but I didn't.

That evening we went out to dinner and he told me that

on his first night at boarding school Clifford had taken Kathleen, wearing a new dress, to a Noël Coward revue. He said he still felt that this had been utterly heartless. It was the most endearing thing I had ever heard about them.

The next day I moved out of Harben Road. Except for John, the house that had held so many growing people was empty.

CHAPTER THIRTEEN

1

When I was a child I sometimes moved into sheds, disused stables, the corners of lofts. I would scrub the floor, furnish them with bits of discarded junk, write PRIVATE on the door, NO ENTRY, KEEP OUT, then shut it behind me and go home to tea. I started life in Aberdare Gardens in much the same spirit, the difference being that I was forty-seven-years old. Looking back on it that seems to me quite elderly; certainly middle-aged, long past the onset of discretion. If my behaviour was 'unsuitable' it seems to me, now I understand how brief and flimsy life is, that almost all behaviour is unsuitable.

Over the next two years all my energies were channelled into one prime occupation: being separated from John. For the first few months, while he was still at Harben Road, we 'phoned each other constantly and met nearly every day. This in itself was far more time-consuming than living together. Returning from some obligatory evening out I would leave a goodnight note on his pillow. One night he was apparently there, but had gone to bed: there was a postcard to Sally and a letter to Jeremy on my desk, a tray of tea and abandoned shoes on the floor. I crept off with my swag of relief and happiness. But when he said 'Come back' I looked away, busied myself with straightening cushions. Stealing was safer.

Both of us behaved awkwardly. He asked me to dinner at Harben Road with one of his women friends. I was glad to see she was plain and dumpy, but scorned the way she sat about while John cooked, not even offering to lay the table. John and I talked about the children, the unfortunate friend looked increasingly dismal. When the meal was over I officiously cleaned up every inch of our kitchen, while they sat on our sofa in our sitting room nervously making small-talk. I swore I would never repeat this experience but my memory was too full, there was no room for it.

'If you were living with someone else,' John said, 'I would begin to court you.'

2

Sally was at school at Frensham Heights, not far from Bedales. Stable Cottage was still unfurnished, so we spent occasional weekends in a country hotel within easy distance of both children. Jeremy was pale and excited, letting his news out cautiously, inch by inch. 'God,' he declared, 'if anyone asked me to stay at home tonight, I wouldn't!' I sneaked into his dormitory and found them running about with their pillows for fighting and their 9 p.m. feast of Polos and Refreshers.

'Have a Polo — I've got plenty of spares.'

'Morty, your ma's here!'

And Sally, now a bottled blonde, mellow, sad, mature, a proper fifteen-year-old. Perhaps, I thought, she's going through her religious time, but without a religion to go through. They knew we were living apart, but didn't ask about it. Probably to them everything seemed the same as usual, until they came home for the Christmas holidays.

It would be the last Christmas we ever spent at Harben Road. John was waiting to move into a flat in Little Venice and the house was already derelict, everything lost or broken, stinking rubbish pushed down the jammed waste disposer, overflow from the bath cascading through a leaking pipe into the front garden, a functioning television set balanced on top of a broken one; if that went wrong another could be balanced on top of it. The dying of the house was too strong for me. I tidied it up as ineffectually as one tidies up the road after a car accident. I slept at Aberdare, getting up at seven to be at Harben Road for breakfast, staying there until they were in bed at night. We took them to *Baron Bolligrew* and *Cinderella*; Jeremy and I plodded round the Elgin Marbles wearing earphones, attached to each other by cable. It was decided that Deborah would live with me and Sally spend her holidays at Little Venice, but neither John nor I could face the problem of where Jeremy was to go in the future. We didn't discuss it and if Jeremy wondered, he didn't ask.

3

John moved out, there was no more Harben Road. So far in our separation I had managed to deal with unhappiness by slapping on a few remnants of bravado, considerably helped by anger. Both now deserted me, or I gave them up as being too difficult. 'No home!' I wailed, so spent all my days driving about, nowhere to hang myself.

I went back to Dr Wollf, more to be in familiar surroundings, safe for fifty minutes, than in an effort to straighten myself out. 'I don't want to be a mess,' I told him. 'It's so uncomfortable, apart from anything else.'

He smiled at that as though congratulating me and prescribed a drug called amitryptolene, which I learned later was recommended for agitated or violent patients and caused 'loss of intricacy in movement or thought, a state of confusion and loss of the libido.' All I knew then was that it made me shake as though every minute were an appalling accident. Dr Wollf took a grave view and suggested a spell in hospital. Hospital? Hospital wasn't home and roses, it was strong tea and dawn and endless hours, rubber sheets whatever the trouble. I went to Little Venice and admired the new bathroom wallpaper. 'Will you live with me in the autumn? My little touchstone, magical Penelope ... It would all be so simple if I didn't love you ...' I have an impression of girls sitting about, plain, good-natured, grubby, wearing down-at-heel sling-backs. John snapped at them and they giggled, making mock-contrite faces.

On 20th June, the day my new novel should have been delivered, there were still only two and a quarter pages. John became Queen's Counsellor in black silk stockings, ruffled lace and a full-bottomed wig. Over lunch one day I brought up the problem of the summer holidays – where would Jeremy be for two months, what should we do? Benign in the dignity of his braided tails, he suggested 'a reconciliation'. 'We're getting on so well,' he said, 'now we don't live together.' To him this seemed to make perfect sense. I felt as though I were going deaf, trying to catch snatches of meaning.

Deborah, now seventeen, was living with me. It was little reassurance to either of us. I found it painful to be watched and watching me made her angry. She attacked her clarinet and slammed doors. I decided to tell her about Randall, though not entirely for the reason I had told Julia about Harrison: Deb may have needed a father, but I needed to unload some blame. He turned up at the flat, fifty-eight-years-old, toothless, weeping, with the head of an old woman. All day he talked and wept and drank and read his poetry, much of it beautiful, and I knew that this was all deeply important to him and that I must try and live up to it, though the gulf between us was unbridgeable. He and Deborah flung themselves into a passionate relationship. I could only think how awful it would be when he died, and how for Deb's sake I hoped he wouldn't die too soon.

On the morning of her nineteenth birthday he came up from Essex to take her out to lunch. Deborah met him at the station, they went to Soho. He reminisced as they walked down Old Compton Street. 'I remember when ...' he said, and collapsed on the pavement. Deb held him while somebody called for an ambulance. She went with him to the hospital, but before they got there he was dead.

4

Reading from the future I can see a monotonously recurring pattern over these years. Directly John went far enough away – but it had to be much further than out of sight; it had to be thousands of miles away – I revived and became cheerful, reliable and competent. I could tell myself that he was simply a man fighting for his freedom and that what he did with it was none of my business. I felt optimistic about becoming a functioning being again and even wrote a few sentences. In August he took Jeremy and Deborah to Greece. 'Sal sings in the bathroom. Tomorrow she goes hop-picking. Why all these months of misery?'

Three weeks later they came back. John brought the children to Aberdare.

'Can I go out to lunch?'

'Yes, of course.'

'I mean – will you be able to give them lunch?'

'Yes, of course.'

'Oh, super! Thanks for being so understanding. See you tomorrow probably ...'

I began shaking again. Jeremy occupied himself trapping wasps. When the jar was full he busied himself with his stamp album. John took us all to the pictures. He held my hand as always, then in the car park the children were divided like Nuts in May and we drove to our separate places. I knew I could only 'win' if he was 'losing', and found that horrible. I couldn't be bothered much with pride, but he managed to turn humility into humiliation and there was no peace offering that he didn't interpret as a sign of defeat. A humiliated, defeated person was someone to hurt with pleasure. John's interpretation was rather different. 'It's funny,' he mused, 'I feel I must for ever be holding you at arms' length, then pulling you to me.'

Both my GP and Wollf were away. I remembered Dr Barrington Cooper, his comforting voice and astrakhan collar. He listened with deep attention, gave me a prescription for 'pretty little pills' and said that I would have to see him regularly. Hyped up by Ritalin, I was convinced that his highly priced concern had saved my soul.

But John went to Hollywood and I forgot to take the pills. Jeremy had a friend to stay, there were huge quantities of chips to fry, expeditions, constant activities. I began to imagine Jeremy going to day school, living with me, learning to take the rough and the smooth of me. Against my better judgement I told him about this; he went to bed carolling how happy he was. Four days later the 'phone rang: 'How are you, baby?'

I went to see Dr Barrington Cooper. 'Indulge me a little,' he said. 'Let's play games. You're not depressive, dear, you're obsessional. Let's try pentathol and methydrine — see what happens.'

'But I'm fine when John goes away. It's just that I can't work.'

'So what difference does it make? Why not try it?'

'It'll have to be after I come back from Montreal.'

'Montreal?' He made it sound like a suburb of Salford. 'What on earth takes you to Montreal?'

'Expo. A sort of preview. A bunch of journalists. They've asked me to go.'

'*Really?*' He was encouraging. 'Do find a nice lover while you're there. We'll play games when you come back.'

Oh warning voice, the day of doom is at hand. But if Barry could cure me of my addiction anything was worth it.

CHAPTER FOURTEEN

1

October 2 1966: Montreal: *What media am I represent-ing? The* Observer *looks neat and disapproving,* The Times *slouches with his 1950's crewcut, the* Evening News *has a lot to say about pop art, there is a young man called Jeremy Hunt and one called Peregrine Long-man, who seems to be Leader or Boss. Geoffrey Moor-house (but who is he? The* Guardian *perhaps?) is the only recognisable human being ....*

That evening I met a slight, dapper lawyer-banker — I was never quite sure which or if, indeed, either — called Philippe Jannes and Moshe Safdie, the architect responsi-ble for the controversial housing complex known as Habitat. Philippe spoke tenderly of his E-type Jaguar and vintage Bentley and offered to drive me to America for lunch, which sounded more interesting than The Theme of Expo, Public Relations and Press Facilities. Safdie's appearance, though pleasant, was by no means remarkable; there was nothing remarkable about him except his expertise and enthusiasm. People who know how to do anything well — build, write, fix machinery, climb mountains, tap dance — are superior beings and I found these qualities irresistible. We drove to the water-front to see how Habitat was reacting to that particular Sunday's sun. Not well, it seemed there was a fault somewhere. Of construction, he said. Of the sun, I said.

'He walked about in a white crash helmet like God directing creation around the 4th day.'

When I returned from an obligatory tour of Ottawa and Toronto Philippe met me at the airport in the Bentley. Two small boys loafed round the car, cautiously touched and stroked it. 'Imagine having one of these, eh? Just to drive around in. My friend says it's bullet-proof.' We changed cars for the E-type and drove towards Lake Champlain. Philippe wore suede, with child-sized Courreges gloves, and drove with much decorum, keeping up a constant, tuneless 'Ta-rum, ta-ra' like a 'bus blowing its horn round Mediterranean corners, for warning, self-protection and the hell of it. I began to feel a flicker in my stomach, growing and spreading until I could hardly bear it, heart thundering, small fires breaking out. I said something foolish like 'If you want to know what's happening, I'm having a novel.' He took my hand, or smiled, or both. I scribbled it down: a deformity (a cancerous breast removed – my scar); the affair with the man who knew; falling in love with a man who didn't. It took half a minute. When we reached the border I stepped out on to America with a finished novel in my hand.

I wanted to buy him a drink, a celebration, a ceremony of drinks. We stopped at a bar in Plattsburgh. It was called Domenico's Cave or something of the sort; there was a mauve room with mauve brick and mauve lighting called The Fascination Room, and a great brawny wrestler – Willy Wall – with huge biceps pounding a mauve grand piano: September Song, Deep Purple. I was wearing Philippe's greenish skin jacket and his pink shirt. We drank neat brandies in ponies, pony glasses, set 'em up

Joe. 'Go back?' he asked. 'Go on,' I said. At the Lakeside Motel, cabin No. 16, there was a vast TV set, a double bed covered in candlewick, bathroom with paper cups on a conveyor belt. The night was accompanied by screaming sweeps of jet 'planes which made us cower, cover our heads, pretend to be in Vietnam. The next morning we drove through forest fires and he told me about the girl he had been going to marry, who drowned in his lake. On the ferry I bought him an object for opening bottles and operating on beavers; a nautical cap for Jeremy. A man in the next car admired the Jaguar; 'Have a good time,' he said , 'whatever your endeavour may be.'

We reached his lake which now looked evil to me, squally and treacherous in the heavy rain. A crowd of people appeared, waving, welcoming him, men in shorts and windcheaters, women in jeans and Irish sweaters, children with blonde, shaved heads. He carried one on his shoulders down to the beach, shoes off, trousers rolled up, and I followed with the women, a slim handsome one called Cunningham, a fat glossy one called Audrey. There was a cumbersome boat lying almost on its side in the water. Cunningham said it was home-built, had a bit of railway track for a keel, could be bought for sixty dollars and belonged to a Member of Parliament; she said it was too heavy for her to steer. The men reckoned that each person could lift 150 lbs, but no one knew how much the boat weighed. Cunningham and another wife carried the mast away, plodding up the beach against the wind. We all heaved. The tractor started, the boat was slowly levered on to the wagon.

Audrey and I went to make coffee. Sorry, she said,

but she hadn't caught my name. I mumbled it. 'It can't be true! Is it true? I've never met anyone famous before, oh dear you must think me so silly, you must think me so gauche. We have a literary circle in Roseberry, all women of course, and we discussed your book and saw the film and we thought the film was dreadful — aren't you married to somebody? — oh my, how stupid you must think I am!' She said she hadn't married until she was thirty, that was why she liked marriage. Of course Peter wouldn't be any the wiser when she told him about me, he didn't read much, he was a Vice-President and doing very nicely.

One by one the men appeared, shining and grinning and quiet, identical as the children. A five-gallon bottle of whisky was produced. The husbands stood at one end of the room, the wives sat at the other talking about schools, the New Mathematics. Pictures of Jeremy were passed round — 'A real Beatle!' they said. One of the young daughters brought them back to me, holding them with stiff hands by the edge, gravely and carefully as she had been taught. Dad Cunningham sat holding his smallest boy, the older child lolling against his legs. There was a great sense of peace and order, refrigerators all cleaned out, cars and station wagons waiting.

Finally Philippe and I started out for his shack. I followed him barefoot, scrambling over lava rocks, boulder to boulder, water and rain, the canvas bag with steak in it slung over his shoulder. At last we came to a hut totally enclosed by trees and water. I stumbled in and fell on the bed. Not a sound. The end of the world. Dozens of French paperbacks. A grey shirt on a hanger, a glass porch hanging over the growling lake. He cooked busily, soft raw peppery steak on an oil stove, one sharp knife quivering point down on the table. I carved our initials in the red paint. I was shivering cold.

In the morning he asked me not to make the bed. I left a maple leaf on the pillow and put on the grey shirt, leaving the pink one on the hanger. He tied the key to a piece of holly and put it under the steps. 'I know where the key is, I know the way in.' We started back through the woods, brambles and branches. Sometimes, he told me, he had seen bears. *I love him for re-creating me. It has nothing to do with being in love, or even with sex which is part of love. The way to lose it all is to cling to it too fiercely. I don't want to let anything else, anyone else, in. My comfort is the idea of writing the novel. My aim to keep alive.*

2

I remember nothing about arriving back in London or the following weeks. We took Sally and Jeremy to Bermuda for Christmas and I remember nothing about that except a picnic on the beach on Christmas Day, a vague sense of eighteenth-century frigates and Captain Bligh. We took them on to New York, stayed at the Waldorf Towers, did the proper things like the Empire State building, Central Park Zoo and the Staten Island ferry, but my only clear image is of Jeremy in an enormous corduroy jacket, bright gold, bought for him by the mother of a schoolfriend of Sally's.

We returned to our semi-separate lives, but it was different, I now had a complete novel to look after. It lay awkward and inert, taking up all the room in my head.

The few thoughts that drifted across its surface were always the same: being alone, not working, being alone. I allowed myself be yanked between Aberdare Gardens and Little Venice, put at arm's length, pulled back again. It was the Law term, no prospect of John going away. If the story wasn't going to die in my head, I had to escape again.

An old friend, Clive Donner, was about to direct a film in Hollywood and suggested I might find it easier to write there. I packed up my typewriter and flew to Los Angeles. He had taken a lavish house on Kip Drive. The fridge contained very little but ice and the whole place was vacuumed and polished each day by a lady who arrived in a pink Cadillac. Clive was in many ways a classic bachelor, austere in his domestic habits, inclined to be fussy; he was busy preparing to shoot, but lived as though he were going to an office, leaving at 8 in the morning, returning by 6, preferring to put on his pyjamas and watch tv rather than go out on the town. He was completely undemanding, always equable. Now my solitary days were put into a context I slowly began to work, hardly daring to believe the sense of peace and contentment. When Clive was there I tiptoed about, desperately trying to be unobtrusive.

The Governor of California — I don't recall which one — had his eye on the property, so we moved to 1426 Seabright Drive, a smaller, altogether more amenable house high above the smog of Los Angeles. It had a garden with oleanders and oranges, a pool. It may even have been approached by a dirt track. For six weeks I sat by the pool and wrote the story of Canada. Apart from that, Penelope Gilliatt took me shopping for pretty

Mexican tat in Olvera Street, I went to Chicago with Gerry Mulligan and sat in a Memorial Chapel while he rehearsed a concert.

'Two before sixty, please ... 1,2,3,4 AND ... I want to hear the 'cellos!'

A little girl with smudged eyes plucked at her 'cello, looking pleased and recognised.

'84 number 2 – we want more separation. Do inject some personality, Marty!'

Gerry bent over his sax, rocked it. In those days, with his golden mane and beard, he looked as though he could split thunderclouds.

On March 1st I sent a cable to my publisher: BULLET-PROOF FINISHED STOP HOME MARCH 11TH.

3

A month later, in Clive's London flat, four Neanderthal boys were sprawling on the sofa, one in an armchair. There was a surly androgyne who muttered about the volume of reduction and a spotty girl in black PVC. They were called The Traffic. Clive, in his pyjamas and dressing gown, was telling them he needed more drama in one of their songs. The loudspeaker at Albert Hall volume was in my left ear.

'If there's a smoothness to the song it may be that one's missing some of the impact?'

The Neanderthals grunted that to them this had been the obvious way of doing it.

'There's so much that's brilliant about it, you just want to sit and listen,' Clive said, conciliatory. 'It's your first happy song.'

'He's going to the chip shop, see, and he's leaving the chip shop with rummy old Linda.'

'Well, we haven't got to write one for the chip shop.'

'Just tell me roughly what the song was — we originally wrote it for the solitude scene — it's got a romantic thing, a folksy thing —'

'Clive's trying to get the meaning of the film out of songs, see? "I wear the crown of a broken clown" —'

'Well, um, I don't know, it doesn't click. My feelings about that lyric are that it's right on the nose.'

Eventually they all shuffled away, and Clive asked me to marry him.

At least I think that was the idea. I was fond of Clive, very grateful to him, but this was no solution for either of us. Secretly, in my illogical heart, I wanted someone to encourage me to go back to John, instead of telling me what I already knew, that it would be virtual suicide.

Dr Barry Cooper was a close friend of Clive's and deeply interested in our relationship. The experiment with methydrine had disappointed him: all I did was lie on his couch in the dark and weep inconsolably while he sat by my side impatiently doling out tissues, waiting for some revelation that never came. Whatever his reason, he suddenly changed tack and said John and I would never resolve the problem of living together until we actually did it. In hindsight he was right, and possibly the result was what he intended. Clive, anyway, was spared certain unhappiness.

I don't remember much discussion or argument. My impression is that John gave in; he certainly made conditions. We would live together, all right; it would certainly be easier as far as the children were concerned. But it would be a rational arrangement. We would lead separate lives. I accepted all this carelessly, not thinking of the implications.

We found a maisonette in Holland Park, far from John Barnes. The rooms were large, ponderously decorated. There was a roof garden edged with a stone balustrade; it was necessary to shout to make oneself heard over the noise of the traffic. In a fit of pliant femininity I had my bedroom papered with roses. John and Liz, his secretary, worked in an enormous, dark study. I think my typewriter was in the sitting room. Sally moved to Holland Park Comprehensive, draped her room in swathes of old curtains, remnants of silk, chiffon scarves. She slept on a mattress on the floor fenced in by a brass bedstead and burned exotic candles. It was the antithesis of Harben Road.

The *Observer* asked me to take over from Penelope Gilliatt as film critic. Brisk independence was called for; this was no time to indulge in hobbies. I bought a number of reference books on Cinema. I would be a career woman tapping to work on high heels, constantly glancing at my watch. *Bulletproof* was published: 'This terrible, compassionate, beautifully written story ...' So that was all right too, thanks to a French banker, a Canadian architect and a little research into breast cancer. I had just paid £300 for my scar to be removed. Attempting a benevolent heart and an expression of alert intelligence, I walked backwards into a new life.

CHAPTER FIFTEEN

1

My greatest wish, not only for this account but for everyone concerned in it, is that I could turn the next three years into hilarious farce; if not that, bitter-sweet comedy, elegantly played; at the very least mild entertainment. There is no point, either for writer or reader, in telling it all as it was, except to say that it was perhaps the nearest John has ever been to hell, a place on which, as a day-tripper, I thought myself an authority.

John was a novice at unhappiness. When it came to manipulating the life he had let himself in for he was all thumbs, his frustration approached agony. *If only I could pick him up and carry him out of his despair. Because I understand his despair.* But my understanding, like Sylvia Plath's, balked at forgiveness.

> .... they pulled me out of the sack
> And they stuck me together with glue
> And then I knew what to do.
> I made a model of you,
> A man in black with a Meinkampf look
> And a love of the rack & the screw,
> And I said I do, I do.

Whatever the situation in my personal life, I was at least spending most of my days among people. I don't know whether they knew how unconfident I was in my role as film critic, how much I felt an imposter with my high heels and notebook. Most of them, anyway, were friendly and didn't comment when I vehemently disliked a movie they all praised or wrote eulogies about something that had them yawning and slumping in their seats. The *Observer* seemed happy. I wrote a screenplay of Galsworthy's story *The Apple Tree* for Warner Bros. They paid, though it was another twenty years before they made the film.

Given half a chance, children are incredibly resilient. Ours survived, perhaps because they were continually kept on the move. Sally, in the thick of it during term time, rode round Notting Hill Gate on an exploding Honda, wearing a crash helmet and drifting chiffon. She wrote poetry, had many boyfriends, danced by herself in the dark. Perhaps her room expressed what she thought of the world, so chaotic that it was almost impossible to open the door, but brilliantly coloured, full of surprising objects.

Madelon was still in Rome, working for the *Daily Mirror*; Caroline, now living openly with Leslie Phillips, making *A Place For Lovers* with Marcello Mastroianni and Faye Dunaway. Sometimes I was introduced as 'Caroline Mortimer's mother', which pleased me. Julia was personal assistant to the agent Denis Salinger and moved into my flat in Aberdare Gardens with a young man known always by his full name, Hugh Fluff Murphy, and Deborah, now on a stage-management course at

Central and constantly headlonging herself into passionate love affairs.

Jeremy's real life was left behind at school; I think the
holidays, at least when he was alone with his parents,
were a kind of uneasy dream. Just after his fourteenth
birthday he wrote his Will:

I shall give my nothingness to nobody.
All shall have equal shares, and let there be no
quarreling over the tiniest bit of non-existent dust.
My house I will leave to nobody, nobody being my
best companion besides you.

3

A great deal of our energy was recklessly devoted to
getting away. I went to the Caribbean with Clive and
wrote a postcard to Jeremy: 'A lot of very old ladies
& gentlemen sitting in their bathing suits under a grey
sky. Longing to come home.' I went to stay with
Clive in Connemara, where he was shooting *Alfred the
Great*, and sat all morning in the middle of a battle
between the Saxons and the Danes, blood squirting
out of polythene cans, David Hemmings thrashing
about in red suede. I took Deborah and Jeremy to
Ireland. In Tramore Jeremy began talking Irish; in
Glengariff we had a picnic in a quiet hot field with flies;
in Waterville nuns were paddling, their habits tucked
up; at Kilcolgan, where *Alfred* was still being shot,
Danes and Saxons were basking in the sun and Clive
explained to Jeremy, who nodded sagely, that he was
trying to *personalize* the battles. We went to a medieval
banquet where the children got tipsy on sangria, and to

the Cliffs of Mohur, which were beautiful and dangerous; on the way to Galway Jeremy suddenly started weeping in the car, explaining that it was something that came over him from time to time.

We rented Yvonne Mitchell's house in the South of France. A lot of people came to stay, among them Harold, Vivien and Daniel Pinter. Daniel, then about ten, broke a cup. He was devastated, refusing to be comforted when I insisted it didn't matter, that it was an ugly old cup anyway and I was delighted to see the last of it. Two years later the Pinters and I met accidentally. We hadn't managed hullo before Daniel said 'I'm sorry about the cup.' I don't know why this impressed me except that like so much else I knew it meant something, but couldn't figure it out.

We took Jeremy and Deb 'on safari' to East Africa. They wrote a detailed 'log' prefaced 'This log consists of 95 pages and 4 clearly labelled diagrams and is all written in handwritten English. This exciting account is well worth reading.' I'm sure it is, but resist it. Although I too saw Thompson gazelles, mating lions, Masai tribesmen and the dentist in Mombasa, their experience wasn't mine. I went with them to Crete and in Heraklion asked Jeremy if he felt superior to women. He said 'Not with you around', dismaying me. On the 'plane back a woman was reading *Pumpkin Eater*. I watched, knowing exactly how far she had got. She yawned, closed the book, dropped it into her basket, combed her hair.

4

My mother was now ninety-two and very unhappy. After my father's death she had been moved, or had offered to move, to the upstairs flat, letting my brother and his wife Jay have the ground floor and garden. Mother and daughter-in-law had hated each other before sight and this was the final confrontation. Fragrant Cloud and Grandpa Dickson were in alien territory. John agreed to contribute to the lease of a garden flat for her in Compayne Gardens, Swiss Cottage — it faced north and was always dark, but the garden was her own. Deborah moved in with her. Identity re-established, my mother quickly came to an arrangement with the milkman and his horse and settled down to a further lifetime of boiled eggs, Sir Kenneth Clark on television and aggressive games of Scrabble with her grand-daughters.

That gives the impression of a cosy old crone, a cottage grandma, and of course she was no such thing. The time of being the Rector's wife, polite small-talk over the teacups, was already forgotten and now she no longer had to keep up appearances for her daughter-in-law or try to placate her son. The longer she lived at Compayne, the more easily she expressed her feelings. They were revealed as insatiable, possessive love, or bitterness that had every appearance of hate. The love was mainly directed towards Caroline, whose birth she had endured — even, by intense identification, experienced. The apparent hate — a strong word, but it has many facets — sometimes darted out in impatience with and disapproval of her younger grandchildren, and always of their friends. Its full strength was mercilessly aimed at my sister-in-law, but as vengeance faded it more and more frequently moved to another target, the one most resembling the original, the Big One, the sixty-four thousand dollar aggravation: myself.

'Hate' may be a misnomer; but when guilt, disappointment and bewilderment are put together it's a virulent mixture. She detested my unhappiness. She thought me vain, selfish, and an appalling mother. By virtue of her enormous age she no longer had to keep a stiff upper lip but, good heavens, I should. She believed unhappy marriages to be a matter of course, men being what they were, so why couldn't I make the best of it? Of course mine had been doomed from the start, but I was always wilful. When you make your bed, you must lie on it; no good kicking against the pricks.

Then there was the incomprehensible 'writing', and now a totally unnecessary 'job'. 'But you don't *have* to work, do you?' she asked, in the same voice she had used to sly poachers and gin-sodden mothers seventy years before. I mumbled some reply, but there was nothing to say. I pretended to fall sleep on her sofa, pretending we were both dead. I gave her five pounds a week, practically her only income. It became, for me, a hopeless relationship.

5

About eighteen months after John and I had set ourselves this trial of endurance, I mentioned to my doctor that I must remember to ring Clive Donner. 'Don't,' he said. Vaguely, I thought it strange. A couple of weeks later Clive told me that he was having an affair with Jocelyn Rickards. I was delighted, sang in the car on the way home and sent a telegram to tell him so. Those were the days of telegrams. They came in brown envelopes, delivered by self-important uniformed lads on motor bikes.

People afraid of direct confrontation, like myself, used them constantly.

I was seeing a lot of Derek Prouse, Dilys Powell's understudy on the *Sunday Times*. Prouse was a typical homosexual of his generation, camp, warm-hearted, spiteful and promiscuous. He was extremely patient with me — though I suspect I was the subject of some scurrilous stories — and kept me amused through many disasters, even coming with me to a remote Welsh cottage after I had split my head open in a car smash, barely raising an eyebrow when I decided to drive straight back to civilisation. His shopping list for this trip still brings a feeble smile: a few women, 3 kittens, 1 goat, 1 boa constrictor, 1 dustbin, 2 fur coats, 1 Vivaldi LP. His greatest tragedy was having to grow old.

I was also briefly buoyed up by the movie mogul Sam Spiegel. He asked us to write a script about Charles Dilke for Rex Harrison and we spent an uneasy few days on his yacht drinking bullshots and 'spit-balling' about the screenplay. I must have known that I, at least, would never write it, but 'spit-balling' is the easiest thing in the world to do, particularly if you're getting paid. I think he took to me because I was sorry for him. I thought he was lonely. Not that I ever said as much, but maybe he felt it and in a perverse sort of way was flattered. I spent a bizarre evening with him during the Cannes Film Festival and when we were back in London he asked me to lunch: 'I wept & wept into his Kleenex under the lace canopy of his guest bed. His sympathy and warmth and bulk brought it on, his warm & generous clasp, the paternal myth ...' When we met again, a few days later, he hinted that money would be forthcoming if I left

John. 'If it weren't for the script,' he said, 'I would want to be as close to you as two people can be.' In fact I resigned from the script shortly after this and never saw Sam again. Sometimes I wonder what would have happened if I had gone home, packed, and presented myself on his doorstep. Looking back I can see there were alternatives during this time, but this one is unimaginable.

Little of this penetrated the insulated wrapping I moved about in when I was outside 73 Holland Park. Once inside all protective covering disintegrated, leaving me susceptible to every draught and creak. There were very few sounds from the outside world. Harold rang:

'Are you ... around?'

'Yes.'

'And ... John?'

'I don't know. I think he's in Paris at the moment.'

'I see ... Well, in that case, may I ... give you a tinkle within the next couple of weeks?'

He sent me his new play, *Landscape*.

The play is beautiful, the definitive piece about non-communication. What do I love about him? The way he writes and looks and talks, though not always what he says. What do I mean 'love'? A strong, tender, admiring affection that needs some sort of physical expression, even if it's just linked fingers over a lunch table. But without his feelings for Vivien and Daniel he wouldn't exist as he does. I more and more respect people who respect their marriages, even though it's sometimes a little sad in a silly sort of way.

Now, in view of all that's happened, it seems very sad,

and not at all silly. Respect for marriage? We might just as well have crossed our fingers going under ladders, avoided passing on the stairs, foretold the future by gazing at old tea-bags.

6

By Christmas 1969 we were barely human. On Christmas Eve we wrapped the children's presents in silence, silently handing sellotape and scisssors. After telling me he was going to Paris for New Year's Eve, John went out. Deborah, Sally and Jeremy set off for Midnight Mass. I arranged the presents round the tree and vacuumed the sitting room while the radio sang comfort and joy.

When Betsy Blair, Karel Reisz's wife, told me that they and the Claytons were going to Klosters for New Year and suggested Jeremy and I joined them it seemed salvation. Jeremy immediately began to ski with much verve and elegance. I looked down the slope, made myself go, panicked, fell in a tangled heap and decided to stay indoors. The Claytons and Reiszes played bridge and were coolly kind, heads of Columbia and Universal played Scrabble. John, having decided not to go to Paris after all, rang every day in a fury of misery, saying he had nothing to do, that it was the most wretched time of his life. On New Year's Eve, at a party of Deborah Kerr's, I suddenly, urgently needed to face 1970 with Jeremy. I skidded and slithered back to the hotel, bought a half-bottle of champagne and raced eagerly to his room. He woke up, glared at me, said he didn't like champagne and humped back to sleep. I have always disliked New Year's Eve and this was no exception. That evening John met his future wife.

He was forty-seven and the fortune teller's prediction was coming true: at last he had found an alternative both to me and to the years of unsatisfactory affairs. 'She's called Penelope,' he said, 'and she smokes Players Medium cigarettes.' *She is 22, a 'model organiser', her father breeds pigs, she has a pregnant sister and is going to America in March ... My heart cracks, but for the first time I try not to show it. Not because I'm afraid of a 22 year old girl, but of John. Of being without him for ever. Very.*

Six weeks later he moved out and I found a house in St John's Wood, near enough to John Barnes. By Easter our marriage was ostensibly over.

CHAPTER SIXTEEN

1

The house in Loudoun Road was a tarted-up version of Harben Road. Perhaps I thought that given enough attention it might reveal the same qualities. The bedrooms were small, owing to the inordinate number of bathrooms crammed into the original structure, but there were high sash windows in the sitting room, a basement ready to be filled with junk, a gloomy dining room. In the euphoria of moving I made jokes: William Morris wallpaper and swagged velvet curtains in the dining room, dangling glass prisms on the piano top, a heavy, fringed table cover, prankish white lace in my bedroom. I instructed a landscape firm to make a Secret Garden complete with swags of rambling roses, tangled ivy and a robin — presumably I intended to provide Ben Weatherstaff and Dickon. Jeremy and Sally came with me. I felt a momentary chill at the thought that they wouldn't always be there — what would it be like letting myself in at night? I'll go round patting the walls, I thought; draw the curtains, see all is right.

For the first few months I continued to do the movie column, but with little enthusiasm. Writing the pieces had been like a stranger's embracing arm, a great deal better than nothing, but now I wanted to get back to the real thing. A.D. Peters brought a bottle of fine whisky —

no more journalism, he said, no more screenplays, just a novel. A few weeks later Deborah started having an affair with David Mercer. The outrageous irony of this catapulted me into writing and I began *The Home*.

The idea was obvious enough:

After 20 years of marriage she finds herself alone with her grown-up children, a relationship revived, all needing, all feeding on each other. A fortress of women in which the young son is the only male. Finally they all go, and she is left alone to face age. The boy hitches to India.

Thank god, I'm alive again. Be careful. Write the book and make the clothes and do the garden and clean the house. All else may fall into place.

The delight was short-lived. John visited frequently, peering round to spot a saucepan he might legitimately claim, uneasy as a dispossessed landlord. 'I think I'll come and stay.' He was as off-hand about Penny as he had probably been about me. 'Oh, she does the rough. I suppose she'll have to go.' I knew it was only bragging, but I carelessly allowed it to feed the poisonous little tumour of hope that still niggled at the back of my common sense. Perhaps all this was part of the elaborate game which someday, far in the future, one of us would finally win; which of us that would be didn't matter, so long as we could finally stop playing. 'I'm sure we'll be together in the autumn,' he said as he left, kissing the top of my head in benediction.

Though neither of them knew it, Wolf Mankowitz had ear-marked Julia for his eldest son Gered, now a professional photographer, when they were both children. Julia married Gered that July, wearing Ossie Clark white and supervised by a beaming Kenneth. The weather was wonderful, a hundred unknown people swarmed over my garden. I remember Sally and Jeremy sitting on the grass, both in flowing velvet, marijuana drifting on the air. There should have been a unicorn, a couple of borzois, a lute or two. John wandered about benignly. For the first time I noticed that he was middle-aged.

2

He 'phoned from Turville Heath. 'What's the matter with Jeremy?'

'Nothing. None of us are exactly ebullient.'

Testy: '*Why* aren't you ebullient?' Penny was talking to Kathleen in the sitting room; I could see my novels and Clifford's gardening diaries on the shelf by the fireplace.

Because it's four-thirty on an October afternoon.

'Don't be unhappy, sweetheart. Let's have lunch.'

I had begun to rely too much on Caroline. *Poor sweet Caroline, I depress her and long not to. I want to be strong and good for her, but I'm like an endless blood transfusion, me getting the blood. Who will save me? I will, no doubt. I'll get some shots from Barry. I'll do something, somehow ...*

At first the shots put feeling in a glass case where I could see, but not touch; by the third day I was wandering through traffic. A few nights later I woke up roaring drunk, *Let's go potty. No no, you can't go potty because Jeremy is coming home for half-term.* I talked loudly, enunciating the words with care, then began to drone, the sound of two discordant notes jammed on an organ. I remembered when I was a child squatting under the laurel bush, called Bath-hound, droning myself into a coma. I'd forgotten how comforting it was. Now I suddenly started shouting for Caroline and realised she wasn't there.

Barry sent his nurse, Roz. She was appalled by my low blood pressure and said it was fatal to eat cheese in conjunction with the shots, a fact which Barry had forgotten to tell me. I was angry. Being unhappy and frightened was bad enough; to be physically ill was unendurable. I had to work, and eat cheese, and live. What was wrong with me anyway?

'Think of it as an allergy,' Barry said. 'Stop seeing John.'

'How can I? He comes to see Jeremy.'

'Jeremy must go to see him.'

'It's stupid to shuttle him about.'

'Do you realise,' Barry asked, his voice stroking the words, 'how masochistic you are being?'

I think he must have changed the shots; anyway they were now called 'boosters'. By the beginning of November I had more or less stopped functioning. I told Barry he must put me somewhere safe for a week or so where I could get rid of the drugs. That evening I lay in bed in the Harley Street Clinic, a small New Zealand nurse sitting guard. What was I doing in bed at seven o'clock in the evening? I had forgotten why I was there. I felt perfectly well. The nurse wrote a long letter, her head bowed as though sleeping.

They kept me drugged the whole of the next day. Deborah sat by my bed reading a book. John rang up, I heard a distant voice saying 'We must all be great friends.' Two or three days later I struggled to the notebook: *Doped literally out of my mind, vaguely realise time crawling by, blood pressure, temperature, pills. This isn't what I wanted.*

I was moved to Greenways, the nursing home where Jeremy had been born and where I had spent the lost weeks ten years before. It was a relief in a way. I understood the early mornings, cups of bitter tea, dear old nurses in tartan shawls; there was a glimmer of comfort in knowing that I would be safe and warm all day, maybe a bit bored, only conscious of the outside world as a handful of pebbles thrown at my window; time and space to explore. John didn't ring. I watched a programme about the Orinoco.

There, at this moment, these people are making their blow-pipes and pounding their leaves and mud, and destroying their deformed children, and sleeping and eating. Now, while I sit in my hot expensive room because I can't bear my hot expensive house, where the light is left on for the benefit of the cats.

John visited, an hour and a half late, bringing champagne, saying he was 'going off to the sun' after Christmas. 'I'll come back and live with you and have a string of girl friends.' 'I love you always.' I made myself get out of bed and sit at the typewriter, wrote six words and crossed them out. Eleanor Fazan, a choreographer and distant friend, came to see me. She and Nigel Davenport were going on location to Kenya in January. She asked me to join them; I was so touched that I wept, embarrassing and alarming her.

Every day after that I forced myself to work on *The Home*. My room grew increasingly chaotic, thick with cigarette smoke; soon, blessedly, the obsession with writing came back and I was happy. Barry said I was getting too high and gave me new white pills. I lay doing nothing, visited by a Baroness with nine names. She was having ECT and seemed to me calmly, rationally mad. I wanted to creep under a bush with my book and listen to silence.

John's mother died the night before the opening of *A Voyage Round My Father*. She had always hated the play and might perhaps have been quite gratified to know that instead of enjoying all the excitement he had to rush off to deal with her remains. I wept a little, not so much for her death — she was very ill — but because I was glad I had known her and that in spite of everything she was fond of me; because the children had given her pleasure and she had been loved, and on the whole had a good life. Why weep about such things?

Barry insisted on giving me a shot that made me half conscious all the following day. *'No work. Nothing sensible.'* Mercer came and stayed for a long time. I wept. I rang Barry and implored him to tell me a funny story. He told me something about Edna O'Brien, which wasn't funny. I wept. He told them to give me a pill, which finally knocked me out. *'My lovely hateful book is my only hope. I can't talk to anyone without weeping. WHAT IS WRONG WITH ME?'*

I remember nothing about Kathleen's cremation except John reading a poem — Emily Brontë I think. They had advised me to take valium all day; that night they gave me three lithium tablets and two Mandrax. I woke up crazy, blundering about and falling over and finally — what dreadful childish humiliation — having to pee on the floor because I couldn't stand up to get to the basin. 'What are they doing to me? Somehow, somehow, I've got to take charge again.'

I started writing as though I had been given a month to live. Deborah organised a house in Cornwall for the Christmas holidays; the day before we were due to go I finished *The Home*: *It's tiny and dreadful and cruel, no more than a crumb of life. But the best I can do. No celebration. Just me and Debby crying our eyes out.* In Cornwall there was snow and sun, a clean house with polished pine, Le Creuset saucepans, a brass door-knocker of a lion's head with a ring in its mouth. Jeremy was there, I know, and probably some of the others. Deborah looked after us.

John came on Christmas Eve. I looked at him and thought how strange, my husband: an overweight, vain, talented man with no idea how to behave or what to do. We ate and drank too much and he gave me a locket. In the late evening we tried to talk. He said that he was only trying to give the children security; that all his problems were negative, the main one being that he got bored so easily. I said very little, too sick and frightened of compromising him and uncertain of the truth anyway. After he left he sent a telegram of thanks and great love. Our solicitors were wrangling about money.

December 31: *It only needs a moment of Julia, whom I see so little, clinging to me and crying, to remind me of responsibilities that are so glaring. She was frightened by my book, by the implied danger to me. I must reassure her. I must be happy and live successfully and show her*

it can be done. I live far too much with my children, and
for their sake, as well as my own, must break away.

3

I went to Kenya. Nigel Davenport was starring in Joy
Adamson's *Born Free*, the place was littered with anaesthetised lions. I remember lying by the pool while delicate
Indians walked by in silk; peacocks crying for help,
herons. We flew to a desert island called Manda, piloted
through thunder and lightning by Dave, who told me he
had read Dunne's *Experiment In Time* at school and
referred to his wife as 'Mummy' — 'I won't be much
good to Mummy tonight.' It was grey and cold on the
island. I shared a tent with someone called Eva. The tent
slapped and the palm trees rattled; a dhow floated across
metal water; an African walked down to the sea carrying
a red plastic bucket. We filed through mangrove swamps
looking for some twelfth-century ruin, Fiz's head bobbing
above the bushes like a little painted marble. There was
Johnny Antoni, in his Bermuda swimming trunks, who
cooked the lunch of raw guli-guli and lobster but refused
to have anything to do with mashed potatoes and peas;
Norman the stills-man and Jill the make-up girl, twice
his size — they held hands, Norman gazing up at her as
though she were the Statue of Liberty. When I hauled
him into the boat from the coral reef where he had
bravely gone goggling there was something about the
wrinkled little man that made me rub him down briskly
with a towel and wrap him up in it, then we rocked
gently on the African ocean talking about his daughter's
O-levels.

No one suspected the flirtation I was having with death. I enjoyed sitting with Dave in the cockpit, flying at mountains, swooping up and skimming their peaks; but although I thought I would welcome crashing vertically into the desert I didn't want to meet a mountain head on. We went somewhere on a boat buffeted by great snarling waves, balanced on the crest, momentarily air-borne, slapped down into chasms of water. I knew that if I let myself fall in I wouldn't give in to drowning, but swim desperately. This paradox, like Daniel Pinter's distress over the broken cup, puzzled me: the enormity of things to be understood.

4

January 31 1971: *I must work, I must run, I must rush, I must persist. There is a shell to be broken, something to plunder. I mustn't sit motionless, but every time something hurts me must be able to move into some more tolerable position.*

Barry came with me to see Dr Kraupl Taylor, an elderly Czech psychiatrist, bright as a gnome, witty, amused, apparently wise. Psychotherapy, he said, was useless without drugs. I dug my heels in, obstinate. Barry was ingratiating and conciliatory, a junior schoolmaster consulted by the Head: come now, we do know what's best for you. I told them my resistance was so huge that a mere aspirin would probably bring me out in a rash. But you do want to get better, don't you? *Who am I to be such an ignorant Puritan? Perhaps I've fallen into evil hands. But I've been through so much that a bit more can't hurt. And perhaps they do know.* I was given Triptozyl and told to attend Dr Kraupl Taylor daily.

February 10: *Kraupl Taylor increased the dose of Tripto whatever it is, though he doubled it only two days ago. He swore I would feel better by the weekend.*

February 11: *Shaking badly, so will cut down the dose. As though it matters. A great effort to make myself get up at 10 a.m. Yesterday I had 2 rums, a Mogadon and 3 Triptozyls for lunch and slept until 6 o'clock. Is that living?*

February 12: *Very little faith in surviving this weekend, or indeed today. I think it's too late for remedies.*

12.50 pm: *Kraupl Taylor recommends ECT. My god, have I gone back to that? He was very sweet, planning his weekend to keep me alive. I wanted to say look, can I just sit in a corner somewhere within sight & sound of you and your wife, and give up, have peace for a few hours. We are meant to have another consultation with Barry tomorrow.*

February 13: *I'm to go back to Greenways for a course of 8 ECTs. I can't bear the idea, but there is no human being to stand between me and it. I can't tell anyone I'm going back, pride is too great. I'm dreaming a nightmare.*

9.50 pm Greenways: *It must be true that depression buggers up the mind as much as ECT, for I can't remember writing that or anything about this afternoon.*

I have a large gloomy room by the front door, very noisy. Am in a sweating cold panic.

Listen: nothing is going to change the situation. John, metamorphosised, isn't going to ride up on a white charger and bear you away. The ECT may produce positive results which will help you deal with the situation. God knows I suppose Kraupl Taylor and Barry are doing their best. I must co-operate and not sink into fear.

February 14: *Came round about an hour ago to the*

realisation that I'm back in Greenways and have got absolutely nowhere. I don't know who my doctor is meant to be.

February 15: *Hutchinsons rang up about* The Home — *say it's stupendous, superlative, marvellous, must win some prize. Life horizontal now. Don't smoke or drink. Pray Deb is in a gentle mood.*

February 20: *They give me electric shocks and I remember nothing. Kraupl Taylor comes and reads* The Times *by my bedside. Barry breezes in. Caroline comes and stays a long time, until I can't make sense any more.*

February 22: *'Don't die,' Julia pleaded last night, crying. 'Please don't die.' So I won't. Kraupl Taylor swears the symptoms, at any rate, will be cured. I don't believe him. My best moment is when I soar away on the pentathol.*

February 23: *Physically healthy, I lie in bed all day, freezing and doing nothing.*

February 26: *Last night I woke up to the fact that I have been a fortnight in this place and have endured five treatments. My sense of time has gone completely. Maybe I should be a bit more outrageous, fight harder.*

March 4: *Walked with Carrie on Primrose Hill. No one knows where Barry is.*

March 7: *Carrie's patience is wearing thin. Kraupl Taylor came for his highly expensive session. The difference between him and Wollf is the difference between a mechanic and someone who believes in the divinity of internal combustion. I reserve judgement about his electric shocks, his Valium injections. As an intelligent friend he is highly adequate.*

March 8: *Though it seems I wrote all that in the far distant past.*

March 10: *John came in the afternoon, once more the story of his love for me & elaborations about where we shall all live. Carrie and Julia prim and cross. They make me feel the whole thing is in very Bad Taste, which it probably is.*

March 11: *Centuries later. Somehow between yesterday and now I've been brought to Greenways, electrocuted. I'm told John, Prouse and Mercer have been to see me, but remember nothing. They tell me I've been in here 'for weeks'. A mutiny of Carrie and Deb. John calling me 'darling sweetheart'. I want to write to Jeremy, not this.*

March 12: *Illegible. Caroline 29.*

March 15: *The sordidness of being ill: the first time in my life when shitting has been like having a baby. In a week now I must totally recover. Plot and plan. A loving letter from Jeremy today.*

March 20: *Today, at last, has been an achievement. A slow, slight crawling upwards. Sorted through the bills, scrambled some eggs for lunch, walked the dogs with Caroline in Regent's Park. And then John came, tired, not happy, moderately sympathetic & concerned, shifty & indifferent about his life. The connection between this man and the miseries of the past few weeks seemed unbelievable. Today my faith began again — in myself, other people, God, what? Now sitting in a clean bed waiting for Julia, & almost hear a grasshopper Magnificat.*

March 28: *John asked me to Turville Heath for the weekend. I'm disgusted with myself; hate every inch of this place where there should be Kathleen instead of Penny with cosmetic blush on each cheek and John marching about in boots being a gentleman landowner. I swear that only I could be so plumb crazy to come at this juncture to a place so full of memories & hurts that it cracks all over.*

April 4: *Loudoun Road I am to go back to Greenways for some new form of treatment.*

April 18: *Greenways: I will not be ill any longer. Perhaps I'm not ill at all. What will Kraupl say if I refuse to be ill? He tells me that although I'm not conscious of it I've been in bed for about 2 months, so it's ridiculous to expect to be physically tough.*

April 19: *Today I leave Greenways for the weekend and Jeremy comes home. I've been lying here for an hour trying* to fight the terror, playing word games in my head, thinking of every trivial thing I can. In fact I'm so frightened that I can hardly write. I know it, but daren't face it, because today I have to do more than just survive, I have to be positive. Kraupl says that for these three days I can 'experiment' with not taking the mid-day Marplan. He also said don't fall out of windows, take an overdose if necessary; but of course he wouldn't tell me how much an overdose is. I'm not going to do either.

April 21: Greenways. Coming back here was the return to school. I cried bitterly. Jeremy leaving seems long ago, but no less painful except in the knowledge that he is clear-sighted and understanding in his way, and remarkably strong. Caroline is pale and tense, not helped by Leslie and certainly not by me following her round like a shadow whenever I get the chance. Kraupl came. He is intelligent, cultivated, and would be a good person to know. But he is not comforting or reassuring. He makes one feel that life is a railway timetable, a map of Greater London, a simple proposition of $a + b = xyz$.

I want it all to be over.

April 23: *Except for Cornwall I have been in this place for 6 months.*

April 24: *For the first time not shaking with fear in the early morning. Don't take anything to excess, particularly relief. When Deb came we went for a walk round the block and met Karel Reisz. He took my face in both his hands but didn't ask why I was in a nursing home or what I was doing walking along England's Lane at 7 o'clock at night in the pouring rain.*

April 25: *I must stop persecuting the children. Scared of the evening, I chased them by telephone — I mean really that I chased Caroline, but both Deb and Sal were involved. If I go on like this I shall do permanent damage. Make a nuisance of myself to other people, or learn to bear being alone, but STOP IT. As usual, I hate everything about myself. As usual, I hate the hating. My mother is unwell.*

April 27: *There's some terrible butchery going on, the nurses hustled me away. I am hemmed in by doctors, by a false and poisonous way of life.*

May 4: *What's happened? I'm bewildered by not being bewildered; know I'm sad but can't feel it; normal, ordinary, average? Somewhere the storm goes on, I know it's there, but hardly a ripple on the surface. Kraupl took me off Optimax & reduced the Nembutal. Says I'm swinging and that's the most difficult time for him. This morning a woman was screaming, shrieking, yelling 'I want to go home!' over and over for what seemed hours.* There is something else to say and I don't know what it is.

May 6: *Penny is pregnant. After the first blow, & tears at being hit — Jeremy is released, I'm released, a burden removed, situation clarified, independence at last, new life beginning [me or the baby?]. Barry told me this morning. I've been talking all day, to Barry, Kraupl, Caroline, Deb, and am exhausted. Kraupl says that tomorrow I shall be desolate. I said we'd bet on it. I wrote to John and asked him if he wanted a divorce, and suggested we discuss it briefly next week. I don't want to meet him and hope that he will reply by letter.*

Kraupl says I'm a remarkable woman. He may be pessimistic, but I think that comes from years of dealing with nuts, & I am not a nut — often. He told me to take a double dose of sleeping pills, [I won't. I already take 7 pills at night], and that if it weren't for 'the life situation' and my personality it would now be plain sailing. It is finally over between John and me. This can't be anything but a relief. I feel myself, for the first time in years — hope, change, a sudden security.

I began to think about work, about writing a tv play for Caroline. I'm liberated, lucky.

May 10: *Alone, and sleeping at Loudoun Road for the first time. I made all cosy for myself so that when I came in it would welcome. The radiator bubbles. I'm glad to be here.*

May 13: *John came round. After all this preparation,*

protection, talk, I was unprepared and alone. He said he didn't particularly want a divorce but Penny doesn't want the child of another woman's husband. Then he complained and waffled about his life, no work, no money. 'But we will always be terrific friends, won't we?' I asked him 'Do you think you're doing the right thing?' He said he was back at the beginning again and no hope, just a placid life. He pleaded 'Come and see me.' I shut the door before he had got into his mother's car. A first step has been taken which I believe straddles John and fear of this house. Now the second, which is work and making sense of the days. And the third, most difficult, finding my kind of people — no one I know now. And the 4th, 5th, 6th ...

May 14: *I collected my things from Greenways & said goodbye, I hope for ever.*

Shortly after this I spent an evening with my mother. When we had eaten our scrambled eggs I plunged in and broached her favourite subject — her death. I said how bleak and desolate I found the prospect of sending her body off to some hospital; that I wanted to give her flowers and the Air on a G string and a grave on the hill at Saintbury. Practical, she said she had cancelled all arrangements for being buried in Saintbury, that by now there would be no room. If I had an alternative to the hospital she would consider it. But I didn't, apart from the supermarket at Golders Green; and the grief burst out while she remained practical. Then, talking of her life, saying how little she felt she contributed, she wept. So there we were. I suppose I wanted to put my arms round her and howl like a child, Mummy don't die. In fact I said the important thing was that I had told her what I felt; what happened when she was actually dead was relatively unimportant. She seemed grateful and touched. Neither of us acknowledged that there had been either rift or reconciliation, but I think she knew and was glad of it.

CHAPTER
SEVENTEEN

1

It had been a curious year since I left Greenways. Predictably enough, I acquired a puppy. She was called Chloe and thumped her tail under my bed at night, a presence. Barry and Kraupl Taylor continued with their various conflicting treatments, but I took little notice of them. Heinz Wollf, saying he knew me too well to take me on again, suggested a psychotherapist in Willesden, a Dr Erskine. When I had mapped my way to Willesden I found a gentle, quiet man in a heavily curtained, nondescript room in a nondescript house. He nodded slowly and said 'Ye-e-s?' in a persuasive way, but little else. I took everything out on him, but it was only when I complained about work that he suddenly snapped, 'Why don't you just write the damned thing and get it over?' Otherwise he coaxed, soothed and infuriated me for many years.

There were good friends, if only I could have recognised them. Frequent weekends were spent with Tommy Clyde, Mary Peach and their children in the country. I slept almost endlessly, contributed nothing. I stayed too lengthily with Clive and Jocelyn, now married and weekending in a rural suburb. Clive sat watching television in his pyjamas, I worked and Jocelyn spent a great deal of time in bed. Assuming that she was a sophisticated, intelligent woman, it never occurred to me how much she resented my visits. I saw Ronald and Natasha Harwood, who lived not far from Stable Cottage, and a great deal of Mercer. I had a number of brief, unmemorable affairs. Emily Mortimer was born. One day I was handed a grubby little Bible, swore I was telling the truth and divorce was graciously granted. John 'phoned. I said, 'You're a free man.' He said, 'Freedom is a very ... word.' 'Loaded'? I don't remember. Four months later Jeremy was Best Man at his father's wedding.

Madelon was now married to Lee Howard, ex-editor of the *Daily Mirror*, a vast hippopotamus of a man, years older than me; he boomed long anecdotes and seemed on the whole benevolent. She had written a funny, neat historical novel called *Darling Pericles* and on its publication day we had a party. Charles was there, stooped and grey, shambling, kindly; his wife, buxom, garrulous Sonia, and their daughter Sarah. Jeremy, his roving eye casing the joint and its possibilities, reminding me of John; Julia pale and silent in brown velvet knickerbockers, Deborah radiant under a pirate's hat stuck with a great red rose, Madelon happy, her huge husband sitting immovable on a sofa, beaming goodwill. It was my debut as mother of grown-up children: proud and satisfied; successfully, I thought, manless.

2

The Home was published in September 1971, the week that all the newspapers were on strike. When I eventually saw the notices they were sympathetic. That book, anyway, was closed. Now what? I watched an old Bette Davis movie — *Now Voyager? Dark Victory?* — and realised what an excellent actress she was before she started doing rubbish. Why not think up a script for her? I wrote care of her agent and received a scrawled, ecstatic reply a couple of weeks later. Her last remaining ambition, she said, was to act with Dirk Bogarde. Very well, I wrote to Dirk Bogarde. He was charming but cautious and suggested I went to stay at a guest house in his South of France village. Much comfier, he said, than staying with him and Tony Forward. I bought him a cow-hide satchel, with no idea whether he would ever use it, and set out shivering with apprehension. Dirk met me at Nice with open arms. Though he was older, more wizened than I had imagined, I loved him on sight. We spent the weekend 'spit-balling' and listening to Judy Garland records. My idea, which was vaguely to do with group therapy, puzzled him. It grew vaguer as time went on. We drove many miles searching for a particular perfume I had bought years before. He rejected the satchel, but started writing fond, comical letters on his bizarre typewriter, which only typed blotched italics. They followed me round the world for many years.

I first met Bette Davis that April in Rome, where she was making some disastrous movie. It was the day before her sixty-fourth birthday. She sprawled on her hotel sofa like a twelve-year-old, kicked off her shoes and drank neat Scotch. 'Gaad!' she said, 'if you could write me a decent script . . . !' I promised to try, though I could see no way of bringing Bette and Dirk together. Both had egos the size of their worlds and Bette, particularly, didn't want to appear fallible.

June 21 1972: *6.30 a.m. Self-trapped in my cabin, New York outside; and suddenly I'm shy and frightened, don't want to go out, don't want to be seen. Ought to be wearing a Good Suit and carrying pigskin instead of milkmaid gingham and Loudoun Road shopping basket. Now stop that. There's no 'ought' and you're P. Mortimer whom everybody loves, except for the people who disapprove and dislike.*

Two independent American producers, Abby Mann and Lester Goldsmith, wanted to make a movie of *The Home* and had brought me over to New York first class on the SS *France*. I was to write the script, Alain Resnais direct. I was determined that Abby Mann and Lester Goldsmith should love me. I would be cool, confident, no trouble as long as they didn't put me in a hotel room with a typewriter.

Lester met met me and to my enormous relief told me that I was to stay with the Manns, anyway for the time being. We drove to the brownstone Abby had rented on East 77th Street, a beautiful, stiflingly hot house full of paintings and *objets d'art*. Abby bore a distinct resemblance to the film star Cesar Romero: slant eyes, flat cheeks, big yellow teeth. I thought him too free with his flattery, but bobbed and was grateful. His wife, Harriet, looked about sixteen and hugged a poodle. I was given a pretty attic looking down on a courtyard, trees heavy with twittering birds. If only I could be inaudible, invisible. I stepped from rug to rug over the polished floors, trying not to make a sound.

Lester flew to Minneapolis; Abby was out most of the

time, and when at home wandered about in a sarong looking abstracted. Harriet took me to Bloomingdales and lunch at the Women's Exchange; we were spared Bergdorf Goodman because they were boarding up the windows on account of hurricane Agnes. At last, after four slightly bewildering days, I met Resnais: professorial, quiet, gentle, elegant in lean blue denim. He not only knew *The Home* by heart, but had already compiled a file on me, everything I had written and much I had been quoted as saying or doing. After we had talked he asked me to write 'a fantasy scene'.

Though I couldn't see *The Home* as *Marienbad* or *Muriel*, I was all for fantasy. I worked the whole of the next day and hesitantly showed the result to Abby. He came plodding up the stairs looking dour: it was no good, I shouldn't even show it to Resnais. When Alain arrived I hid in the kitchen with Harriet, talking about clothes and recipes. Resnais had warned me that he never showed any enthusiasm and after Abby's verdict I was prepared to fly back to London in the morning; but 'Perfect!' he said, '*Extraordinaire!*' and kissed me on both cheeks. Abby made the best of it, but I don't think he ever forgave me.

A few days later I sat in a boutique watching Harriet trying on Buz Berkeley clothes while her mother exclaimed 'Oh, funky!' 'That's adorable, Hatty!' I smouldered with anger. What was I meant to be doing in this tenth rate Biba? Supposing I were a man writer? I wanted to work, but both Abby and Lester were evasive. Resnais, they said, was unavailable. I was contracted to get quite lavish expenses, though living with the Manns I didn't need much; nevertheless I had run out of cash, which was humiliating. 'Isn't that cute?', 'Great outfit!' I made some excuse and rang Resnais from a call box. 'I have been waiting to hear,' he said anxiously. 'How are you working? Are you well? What is happening?'

Ten days after my arrival I took the miserable poodle for a walk as far as Park Avenue; it was another day when I didn't know what I was meant to be doing. Harriet was suddenly 'ill', going perkily off in her new outfit to the doctor. Abby emanated such lugubrious tension that it was hard to be in the same room or house, those too-even yellow teeth bared in mirthless welcome. I supposed I could go to the Museum of Modern Art, sit in the sun and read Emily Dickinson, but was that what I was here for?

I went to the Museum of Modern Art, but Alain came with me. We sat in the garden for two hours talking about the script, then went to see films at the Italian Exhibition. As we sat there I thought, my God, I'm watching films with Alain Resnais. The final dregs of the past ten years seemed to drain away. I was awe-struck at my good fortune.

4

It's odd, but I can't recall what Lester Goldsmith looked like. I know he was small and dark, the sort of man who expects women to talk in a sexy murmur, regardless of what they're saying. I agreed to have dinner with him, thinking I could bring up the question of my expenses. He promised me a cheque in the morning and suggested going back to his apartment where, he said, he had some great records. I should have known better, but Lester had said he was my 'very good friend' and the prospect of returning to Abby was even less appealing. As I was tussled with on the floor, trying to avoid his brandy breath and lacerating moustache (ah, he had a moustache), I thought angrily of the months of work ahead; I very much wanted to write the script, but not if it entailed keeping a lecherous film producer happy. I shoved him off and bolted into the rain. No cabs. I had a key to 231 East 77th, but tonight the door was double-locked. I rang and rang until Abby appeared, blinking in his sarong.

I was being a nuisance, but what to do about it, where else to go? The last thing I wanted was to inflict my doubts on Resnais. There was Joe Fox, my publisher at Random House, but while in London he had always been a dim figure, here he was tanned, rich, successful, in a beautiful apartment with onyx chess pieces and *Traviata* on the stereo. He had told me that though he loved his wife desperately they were getting a divorce, and talked lengthily about his emotionally disturbed son. It was all too familiar and made me uneasy. Bette had asked me to stay in Connecticut, but she had been so drunk on the 'phone that I dreaded it. Rachel Mackenzie was very ill. Penelope Gilliatt was effusively friendly, but I couldn't cope with her desperate greed for love. Gerry Mulligan, now living with Sandy Denis, was fond and generous, but in a different world. We wandered along Broadway at one in the morning; they loaded me with records, cassettes, the five volumes of Leonard Woolf's autobiography, and I couldn't bear to spoil it by telling them that I suspected I might be in trouble. The only other friend I had in America was a painter called Daniel Lang, but he too would make irrelevant and time-wasting demands. All I wanted was to be left alone not alone, to work and breathe unheated air. It seemed an extraordinarily difficult thing to realise.

One night Harriet's cousin Dick joined us in a Spanish restaurant for a dreadful meal of rice and dead lobster. I had left my doorkey behind, assuming Abby would have one. He didn't, and blamed me. We stood on the doorstep while he screamed, literally frothed at the mouth. Finally he scribbled his secretary's 'phone number on a scrap of paper, threw it at me and bolted into the night. Harriet had disappeared. Dick walked me to a call box and rang the secretary: a crackle of abuse told him he had the wrong number. It was two o'clock in the morning. I was wearing a chiffon dress and a scarlet feather boa. We caught the subway and walked to Dick's room on East 4th Street. It was at the top of many flights of stairs littered with squashed beer cans and unrecognisable refuse, the walls sweated and the smell was appalling. The room, about three metres square, contained a truckle bed, a table, a chair and a rusty electric hotplate. Dick offered me the bed and lay down without pillow or blanket on the floor. Everyone else in the building seemed to be having parties. I stared at the cracked ceiling, expecting it to collapse at any minute, and thought of rats and cockroaches. Sleeping or waking, despairing nightmares were the same. Sometimes Dick would ask 'Are you all right?' and I answered, 'Fine. Are you all right?' Towards dawn, Buddhists started chanting in the next room. Dick made pale tea in which he dropped a wedge of old lemon. We drank it out of the only mug, silent and shivering, then I pulled on my dress and soggy feather boa and left. I didn't have the faintest idea where I was and walked until I found a call box. I had no money, so reversed the charges when I 'phoned Abby to tell him I was going home that day. His apologies were so grovelling and my discomfort so great that I weakened.

Nevertheless, I knew that if the script was ever going to be written I must get far away from both its Producers. How I was going to do that was still a mystery. Bette Davis provided the answer. I found her in a shadowy, low-ceilinged clapboard house by a stream, wearing white trousers vaguely reminiscent of the pedal-pushers of her heyday and a white jockey cap; the bulging blue eyes, the bowless upper lip, the disdainful sneer and rasping voice were the same as they had always been, but she was old and hating it. 'Ten years!' she snarled, pouring a treble whisky. '*Ten years* since I had a fuck! What d'you think of that?' She was never still, up and off, back and forth, dusting off crumbs, plumping cushions, straightening pictures. A lot of kitchen work went on, cooking, tidying, stacking, swearing. The house was full of beautiful old American and French furniture, photographs of Franklin Roosevelt, Churchill, Kennedy: 'I'm the only darn' Democrat in Westport!' Starved on rice, I ate gluttonously at dinner. We both went to bed at nine-thirty. Bette, in white silk pyjamas, flung my bedroom door open and wedged it firmly, saying I could now hear the stream and dream happily.

She was very enthusiastic about *The Home* and wanted to play the agonist's mother, Mrs Bennett, a character I had vaguely based on my own mother, though Mrs Bennett lacked her imagination and sense of doom. I could see that Bette, descended from a Boston matriarchy, blue-blooded but down to earth, would probably steal the picture. I told her everything about the situation except my suspicions about Mann's and Goldsmith's competence. 'You've got to move out,' she said. 'Don't worry, I'll find you a house. Godammit, this script is *important*!'

The next day was the Fourth of July. Bette had asked three elderly girl-friends to dinner, all of them patriotically dressed in red white and blue, all of them tipsy, giggling or shrieking according to their natures. Someone had brought huge, damp sparklers from Georgia. I shall always remember Bette in confederate costume, a stars and stripes jockey cap, trying to light the unlightable things. It was a macabre and enjoyable evening.

She was very frightened of herself, or of the old woman she was trapped in. One evening she asked me to answer the doorbell. A small girl standing on the doorstep clutching two gladioli took a deep breath: 'Please will you give these to Miss Davis, because she is so beautiful.' I thought surely Bette would thank her, but she refused to see the child and threw the flowers in the trash. She was desperate about her appearance, tormented with indecision about whether to have her face lifted; on the other hand she made a point of telling everyone she was sixty-four, and even Bette couldn't expect them not to believe her. Then the make-up would go on, the eyelashes, the toupee, the straps, the corset, and her mood soared, she could glitter and dance until the performance ended and everyone went home and there she was again, a few hours nearer death.

Her daughter, known as BD, lived not far away; she

was married and had a small boy, claimed by Bette to be the apple of her eye. Her relationship with her daughter and son-in-law seemed predictably stormy, though nothing compared with her relationship to her own mother. It was easy to persuade her to talk about this, difficult to make her stop. One day her mother would be malicious, cruel, the source of all the evil in Bette's life. 'I bit her!' she crowed, 'I bit her on Eighth Street!' The next day Mother would be transformed into an angel, her death the greatest tragedy. She didn't talk about herself, not as most people do anyway; there had never been a self apart from Bette Davis the actress. She could talk about her indefinitely and I loved to listen.

Before I returned to New York, Bette had indeed found me a house, a Grandma Moses cottage owned by a meek spinster who arranged food for photographs in glossy magazines. I could rent it until 29th July. It appeared that practically all the women in Westport were estate agents, perhaps finding this a suitable profession to take up when their own homes became empty of husbands and children, and they were all in awe of Bette. There would be no problem, she said, in finding a second house. She had to be in New York to do a Johnny Carson show in a couple of days and would pick me up and bring me back with her.

I returned to East 77th Street to find that Abby's nephew, a fifteen-year-old drop-out, had been sleeping in my bed. I changed the sheets and foolishly rang Lester. He didn't seem abashed by my rejection of him; in fact he was so sympathetic that I confided about the nephew and told him that Abby frequently sniffed white powder from a snuff box. Snuff wasn't white, was it?

Was cocaine white? I didn't know, never having seen any.

'You sound so upset,' Lester said. 'I think I'll come over right away.'

'No, no, I'm fine. No really. It's just that ... well, I'm a bit scared of all that. I feel better now I've told you. Don't say anything to Abby, will you.'

'Of course I won't, honey. But you'd feel even better if you talked it out.'

'No really, Lester. I'm going to bed.' I rang off. But I was afraid of Abby and locked my bedroom door.

The following morning Abby bellowed to me to come downstairs. I found Lester, looking smug, in the sitting room. I had made libellous statements, Abby yelled, about him being a drug addict. I told him not to be ridiculous. I had simply told Lester that he sometimes sniffed white powder from a snuff box, which was true. Maybe it was aspirin. They both became hysterical. When I yelled 'SHUT UP!' they stopped abruptly in mid-scream and stared at me, their middle-aged men's faces blank. I said that unless they gave me the money they owed me I would resign from the script, and walked out. Up in my bedroom I shivered and wept a little.

With ill grace, Abby produced a cheque for $500, saying he didn't know how I was going to cash it as his bank was in California and he had no arrangement in New York. He then left for Fire Island, wearing his 1950 Hollywood costume. Lester had swiftly departed for Minneapolis. I rang Joe Fox and asked if he could cash the cheque. He was doubtful, apparently having to consult Wall Street before he could part with five hundred dollars. A couple of hours later he rang and said the money was sirening over under armed guard. I packed and waited for Bette's car. It arrived, the size of a small room, equipped with bar, television and musak, driven by an enigmatic chauffeur. When we picked Bette up she was wearing straps, a toupee and, in spite of the weather, furs. Once inside the car she stripped, furs first, then toupee, then straps, finally shoes. She poured herself an outsize whisky and lay back wriggling her toes. 'Gaad! What one goes through for the sake of one's Art!' I wasn't the only one making a getaway.

By the time we reached Westport and the Grandma Moses cottage — whimsically called 'Hillan'dale' — Bette was herself again, staggering a bit. She produced a lavish picnic, made lists, told me what to eat and drink, showed me how the dishwasher worked, broke a number of plates, swore a great deal, prepared me a supper of southern fried chicken, told several scurrilous stories about Joan Crawford and finally left. I didn't know what I would have done without her. I didn't know what I was going to do with her either.

Late that night the 'phone rang. 'I just thought you'd like to hear the 'phone ring,' Bette said, and gently replaced her receiver.

5

Lester had agreed to pay the rent and give me a living allowance; now, possibly contrite, he offered to pay Julia's fare and $120 a week to type the script as it progressed. This was probably no more expensive than putting me in an apartment or hotel in New York and

Abby, certainly, was glad to be rid of me. I fixed up a table in the garden and started work at last.

A few days later Joe Fox telephoned, very embarrassed: Abby's cheque had bounced. I told him that Anthony Jones, my agent, was on his way to New York and would undoubtedly sort it out. I was light-headed with freedom, work, the prospect of Julia coming. Bette had fixed credit accounts for me at all the local shops, though I had no hope of paying their bills. Lester was in California and Abby drowned on Fire Island for all I cared. I wrote to Resnais and told him I was doing well.

Julia arrived and industriously set to work, taking time off only to do her yoga exercises on the lawn. I was a little apprehensive when she said Gered was going to join us, Hillan'dale being small and not really suited to domestic life, but in the meanwhile our typewriters clacked at either end of the garden, we lived on salad and cheese, the sun shone.

The food-arranger had lent me her car, a battered Buick. I drove it round to Bette's. She was looking very old that day, knobkerry legs under a split caftan, toes covered in corn plasters, tight green headscarf to hide the balding hair. Glaring at the car with disgust, she flung open the trunk. 'My Gaad!' she screamed, 'I don't *believe* it!' and began clawing at sodden mounds of old news-paper, mouldy straw hats and shoes, flat tyre, sacks of some sort of mulch. Soon everything was thrown on the driveway and a gardener summoned to get rid of it. 'I've never seen anything *like* it in my life! I don't *believe* it!' she kept exclaiming for the rest of the evening. The state of the trunk was obviously something to hoard up and relish until the poor food-arranger returned from holiday. There was no longer anything big enough in Bette's life: she was forced to treat a speck of dust, a creased cushion, a yawn or thoughtless platitude as a major outrage. There were no preliminaries to her attacks, no gradual warming up; the most she needed was another whisky to set her off: '*Gaaad*! ...' People were frightened of her. I wasn't and perhaps that was the reason she seemed to like me. She approved of Julia because she didn't get in the way but lowered herself cautiously into the 'swimming hole' and swam round and round, slowly, with dignified pleasure.

6

My son-in-law Gered was — is — a photographer, specialising in rock groups and showbiz personalities. He arrived sniffing the Connecticut scene for contacts, ready to hustle. We had to leave Hillan'dale anyway, so moved into a much grander property, White Birch, a one-story Californian-style house with a large garden. I continued work with hardly a pause. The situation with Abby and Lester changed dramatically every day. On Thursday they said were coming to see me on Monday; but by Monday Lester had disappeared and Abby taken sole charge. He would come on Wednesday, bringing $1000. On Wednesday he rang to say that Arthur Hiller was anxious to direct *The Home*, therefore he was too busy making a deal to come to Westport but was going to double my percentage. He didn't say how he had explained this to Resnais, and in any case I didn't believe a word of it. Anthony Jones could only suggest that I returned to England until the whole thing was sorted out, but the script was two-thirds finished and although there were dozens of bills and no prospect of paying the rent I was living my ideal life, or as near to it as I could imagine, and nothing would persuade me to change it for Loudoun Road. If nobody else was going to solve the financial situation, I must. I cabled the bank to send everything left in my deposit account.

By the end of that week Abby had vanished. I was now working entirely for myself. Steve Sheppard, Resnais' agent, came up from New York; he was an emotional young man, but although his enthusiasm about the script sounded a touch excessive it was clearly genuine. He went back and rang David Susskind. Susskind insisted on seeing the script immediately, but it wasn't finished and I didn't think it would be for weeks. Suddenly I found myself embarking on a two page speech and as the last line was written I could see freeze on close-up, crescendo strings, The End, titles rolling. Julia typed in a frenzy; next day Gered delivered it to Susskind, who didn't like it.

I can't remember how, but through some machination I managed to contact Robbie Lantz, a top agent in the movie world — an immaculate, silver-haired gentleman given to sending lavish bouquets to his female clients, who were, I imagine, few. After reading the script Lantz took me over, delighted at the idea of Bette's Mrs Bennett; it was obvious, he said, that Paul Newman should direct and play the husband, Joanne Woodward the wife. Bette thought this a great idea and immediately scrawled them a note. Joanne rang and asked me to go round for a drink — apparently they were my neighbours.

Together with ten million other women, I had dreamed for many years of meeting Paul Newman, though in rather more exotic circumstances than Westport, Connecticut. Now it came to it I felt curiously reluctant, tempted to go down with measles or suffer a sudden bereavement.

Julia and Gered left, Caroline arrived. I met her at Kennedy with a nonchalant, 'We're having a drink with Paul Newman tomorrow,' and heard her heart sink while she said in her actress voice, 'Oh really? How nice.' Bette, at her most charming, came to supper and told us of the savage injuries she had received from being clasped to Joan Crawford's bosom in *Whatever Happened To Baby Jane*. 'Solid steel, my dear! Lacerated!' She admitted that she had made a date to have her face fixed in California. 'You're mad,' I told her. 'Your face is your fortune.' But I could understand how she felt. I too could do disastrous things to myself.

The following evening Caroline and I spent a long time making ourselves look as though we had taken no time at all and took a copy of the script to the Newmans. We sat round a long table on a vine-covered porch, Joanne lay on a chaise-longue in the shadows. She was beautiful. He was beautiful. There was a bald, gentle writer, Stuart Stern, who talked about some writers' colony called Yaddo. I don't remember anything the rest of us said. We were asked to stay for hamburgers and sweetcorn. Paul made the hamburgers; like many men, he somehow managed to give the impression that his cooking was a subtle insult to his wife. She lay palely, radiantly smiling. The script was barely mentioned. When I urgently asked Paul to read it his intensely blue eyes became almost tender and he murmured 'I will ... I will ...' as though abstractedly soothing a baby.

Joanne rang next morning saying she liked it very much, but didn't want to play another distressed wife. So that was that. Caroline and I drove off to Boston and New Hampshire, stayed for a few days in a log cabin on Silver Lake and came back to find that every one of Abby's and Lester's cheques had now bounced, including those for the rent. Robbie Lantz, a little more brisk than usual, promised to take care of it until they could be tracked down. Bette 'phoned at three in the morning. She had decided not to have her face done and was celebrating. I congratulated her warmly, declined her invitation to breakfast and said goodbye. 'Never say that! Never! *Au revoir ... au revoir ...*' I had a dreadful feeling she was crying. I packed up script and typewriter, sad to leave, apprehensive about England.

The remaining history of *The Home* can be brief:

September 12 1972: Otto Preminger has bought a 6-week option for $3000. If he can get Elizabeth Taylor he will make the movie for an over-all payment of $100,000 and 5% of the gross.

September 13: Resnais rang, wanting to talk 'for three or four days'. I told him about Preminger, but he was relentless.

September 20: Elizabeth Taylor wants to do the movie.

October 7: Paul Newman rang from Ireland. I asked him to supper on Tuesday but of course he won't come.

October 10: Resnais to lunch. We walked Caroline's dogs and Chloe over the sullen Heath.

October 11: Preminger at the Dorchester was most genial. In spite of not being able to sell it to 'the majors' he seems confident of doing it. He goes to see Elizabeth Taylor in Munich tomorrow.

Paul N. had rung, so I rang him back. Cold or shy, who knows, I never will. He starts shooting tomorrow with only two thirds of a script.

October 19: Preminger fallen through.

October 25: Negative news from Steve Sheppard. I begin to doubt whether the picture will ever be made.

It wasn't. I have no idea whether A. D. Peters ever traced Abby Mann or Lester Goldsmith, but they footed the bill, which was considerable.

CHAPTER EIGHTEEN

1

When I returned to London I found that legal proceedings between John and myself were still dragging on nine months after the divorce. His attitude was simple: 'Why should I support you when you're not there to cook my dinner?' Mine, less immediately convincing, was that he owed me, not for services rendered, but for emotion wrongly expended, obsessions maintained, hopes kept simmering, fantasies believed. My QC puffed hungrily at an unlit cigarette; when the tip became soggy he dropped it in the wastepaper basket and took out another. My junior wore hand-knitted socks, his shirt cuffs were frayed, he wound legal tape round his fingers until he had fashioned a perfect rose which he placed neatly on the edge of the desk. My solicitor was a big, shiny-faced man with a dry sense of humour. They all sat round discussing me. 'She is fifty-four,' the QC said, 'and of course she doesn't remarry and is a widow . . .' 'Quite, quite,' the solicitor agreed emphatically. I listened, feeling a tired eighteen. But I was fifty-four, without security and liable to be a widow. I felt a strong urge to say 'All I want is to gossip with John and be kissed occasionally by young men with warm mouths', but in fact I said nothing.

At absurd conferences with our rival lawyers we

spoke to each other in code, secret allusions, private jokes. John suggested I should become his tax free literary adviser. The lawyers, like undertakers at a wedding, were suspicious and disapproving. From time to time we would meet and make straightforward agreements between ourselves which would later be qualified and elaborated by solicitors until they were unrecognisable; then hostilities would begin again, painful, wasteful, pointless. Unless John was getting it all free on the principle of dog doesn't bite dog I can't imagine why he bothered. Perhaps he thought it the correct procedure. Perhaps it was a way of keeping in touch.

2

Each time I came back the gap I had left behind seemed to have grown smaller, more difficult to fit into, its surroundings more alien. Loudoun Road, in spite of all my efforts, had never become home. The jokes rapidly palled. Expensive shrubs and climbers refused to burgeon, the patch of garden to be secret. Everything I had put in the house looked uneasy, as though it was being stored. Only the livid green and pink bathrooms were permanent, sickening with the metallic smell of hot water, ventilated by a contrivance that roared when the lights were switched on. I'm not sure what kind of people the house needed; a pop group called The Hollies lived next door and seemed pleased enough, but it never warmed to me.

Over the years I had been going to Stable Cottage fairly regularly. It had restored my sanity during the Holland Park era and was more familiar, worn into a more comfortable shape, than Loudoun Road. The grass was ragged, the garden flowered with weeds, but I only went there for pleasure, and pleasure is what I usually found. Now I began going there even more frequently. When I woke in the mornings I always felt, illogically, that something remarkable might happen during the day; there was always the chance of seeing Jeremy, and Bedales itself gave the drab little village a certain liveliness. There was a pub with a beautiful unkempt garden in which one could sit long into a Saturday afternoon, drugged with the sound of bees and smell of honeysuckle; a bookshop a mile away in Petersfield, tottering floor above floor of yellow-paged, mouldy treasure; a barn full of remarkable junk, where I bought a harmonium. Jeremy, now seventeen, had spent nearly half his life in these surroundings and knew every footpath and short cut. Though he looked wild with his shoulder-length hair and ragged clothes, he seemed to me at this time gentle and studious. *Jeremy here, great pleasure, particularly when he sits and reads Ezra Pound and I sew and the afternoon drifts safely by. He goes in and out of my life, but never my solitude. That seems impregnable.*

I began a novel called *I Bit Her On Eighth Street*, one of those ideas that seem at first as though they could be written in a week, and probably often are. As usual, fiction defeated me. I didn't know my characters, couldn't rely on their responses, imagine their memories or their futures. It amused me for a while before I got bored with it. But another book had been nagging me for years, though it had been blotted out in the Holland Park period — a swan song, a huge, rambling story told by a grossly fat old woman I called Agatha. Everything I had ever thought, felt or experienced would go into *Agatha*, except that there would be no children. In this way I might discover the person I was before I married Charles; the person I needed now my tenuous thread with the future was broken. I was desolate when all that emerged was the same slick prose, every emotion fined down to a pinpoint, every howl reduced to a murmur. Even so, I believed the book could be written, would someday be written. Meanwhile I accumulated every detail of life and stored it, hoping to match it up with something in a forgotten past.

But hoarding and brooding wouldn't pay the bills. Having gambled everything on *The Home*, I was living on credit. The few brittle chapters of *Eighth Street* and a hopelessly inadequate synopsis of *Agatha* were fattened up by agents and I was shipped back to New York to be auctioned. In my room at the Algonquin there was a white azalea from Robbie Lantz with the message 'Welcome to New York — it's the home for you!' For me? Which one, the writer with the price tag or the woman irresponsibly pottering round Stable Cottage? I could only understand a life that generously included work. That life was over. What I had to confront now was work that imposed a way of life. I knew the time had come to make a choice, but how to choose between two people in one body, sharing one history?

For ten days I lunched and breakfasted and drank with men in suits and one or two worried women. I had a slight cold in the head, snuffling and feverish, and between breakfast, lunch and martinis spent a lot of time sitting on my bed, hollow-hearted, separated from *Agatha* and all I considered real. The one thing that cheered me was that when it was over I was going to Westport to stay with Bette.

She sounded excited as a child with a treat in view. My, she would be glad to see me! Did I like goose? She would stuff a goose, she would make a syllabub. When at last the final Saturday arrived I packed with joy and rang her to say I was on my way. She couldn't wait, had been up cooking since seven o'clock. 'I've got a bit of a cold,' I said, 'but I won't breathe on you.' I finished packing and gave the azalea to Jack MacGowran, then living at the Algonquin. The 'phone rang just as I was leaving.

'Gaad, it *kills* me to have to say this, but I just *daren't* have you up here with a cold!'

I couldn't believe it. 'But Bette, it's not —'

'I just can't risk it, dear. I'm devastated , but — '

I rang off. In a cold panic, I 'phoned an interior decorator in Bridgewater. He was very alarmed and said he was going out to dinner and didn't think . . . 'That's fine,' I said, 'I'll boil myself an egg.' The poor fellow had no option. It ended with him playing Noël Coward on a white piano until three in the morning. I never spoke to Bette again and it wasn't until I saw her interviewed on television shortly before her death — a tiny, antique skeleton, the straps tightening the remains of her face, eyelashes ghoulishly stuck over sunken eyes — that I finally forgave her.

3

Doubleday won the auction and Allen Lane bought me in England, but until I received an invitation to stay for two months at Yaddo, the writers' colony in Upper New York State, I very much doubted whether I could actually write the books. With no idea what Yaddo might entail beyond being cared for, no responsibilities, nothing to do but work, I arranged to go there the following July.

Meanwhile I was at least able to pay the bills and supply Jeremy with necessities he didn't want. He had won an Exhibition to New College; meanwhile he was living in the Loudoun Road basement with Polly Fisher, a girl he had met at Bedales. Shortly after he went to Oxford, Polly's father became President of Wolfson. The Fishers' house in Oxford was full of music and galoshes, books, flowers and the penetrating sound of upper-class women's voices, the antithesis of Jeremy's home life, whatever and wherever that was. Perhaps I felt he preferred it and was only using Loudoun Road as a convenience. Perhaps I was right. My relationship with him at this time was, I suppose, typical. I went through periods of thinking him callous and selfish: he left the bathroom in a mess, wouldn't so much as wash up a cup, he was uncivil, he broke my heart. What he thought of me I don't know, it was all mumble and mutter and dark looks, then mutual forgiveness.

I was relieved to be alone with Chloe at Stable Cottage. *My solitude is peppered with visits, people coming as though they were students come to examine a rare disease. They learn something, perhaps. I remain unchanged. I cook, I entertain, I'm P. Mortimer, self-sufficient, funny, astute. But oh, when they go. And when they're here. And before they come. Underneath, there's all that ever was, but so well hidden that I often can't find it myself.*

185

4

Deborah and Colin were married at the Hampstead
Town Hall that November. Humphrey Swingler, Randall's brother, came to the wedding. I had been more
than a little in love with Humphrey in the black and
white past, long before I met Randall, let alone John. In
those days he was careless, light-weight, charming, my
brother's greatest friend, and lived in a gaunt, ramshackle
house on Primrose Hill with his wife and two daughters.
I often visited them with Paul, but in my memories
Humphrey is always slightly drunk, on the spree at the
Gargoyle, the French Club in Little St James's Street,
the 'Winch' in Swiss Cottage. We danced for hours,
looking into each other's eyes and smiling. He went to
South America with Laurie Lee and the film unit and by
the time he came back I was in love with his elder
brother.

Supposing he hadn't gone to South America? There
might have been no Deborah; possibly I would never
have met John. As it was, Humphrey's wife and one of
his daughters committed suicide and he married a cheerful
girl called Pam, who bore him a second family. Now,
after quarter of a century, this family sat beside him
while Humphrey, held together by surgery but still raffish
and slightly drunk, watched his niece being married.

Judy, Randall's eldest daughter, came with her husband. She had every reason to resent both me and
Deborah, so this was a generous act of forgiveness. Paul
was there with my still remarkably pretty sister-in-law,
an avuncular mask clamped over his normally grim
expression. I ask myself why I haven't written more

about Paul and the answer is that although he is in my thoughts and heart now, he wasn't then. The time for writing more will come when it is ready.

John was there. He had been Deb's first visitor in the Henley nursing home and had endured her frantic squalling in King's Bench Walk, put up with her habits of shitting in the Temple car park and beating Judges' Daimlers with large sticks. Deb was fiery tempered and as she grew older they had savage fights, nails, teeth and the flat of John's hand. Their affection for each other never seemed disturbed by these ructions. John loved people who bounced through life scattering good will, undistracted by futile searchings for whys and wherefores; although he adored Sally he had more in common, I think, with Deborah. Now he attended her wedding looking portly and benevolent, his wife Penny wearing a little woollen hat.

Deborah and Colin were living with my mother. That morning she pushed a note under their door inscribed 'Hail Happy Morn' but didn't come to the wedding, saying she had nothing to wear and buying a new dress would be a foolish investment. Her day must have been spent as usual, hands folded on her lap, watching the slow panorama of ninety-four years pass behind her eyes, perhaps thinking with renewed hope of a great-grandchild. She had already become an absence to us, but since she was still alive that absence couldn't be accepted or understood. I don't think we even noticed she wasn't there.

Jeremy was Best Man or, in register office parlance, Chief Witness. In spite of the seven years difference in their ages Deborah had always been his favourite half-sister; they had walked the Pennine Way together, hitched to the South of France, shared tents in Greece, straw huts in Africa, innumerable hotel bedrooms. Sally, Julia and Gered came, but Caroline was acting Eva Braun to Frank Finlay's Hitler and Madelon was still in Rome. Colin's family, though equally involved, were as much strangers to us as we were to them. We smiled at each other like guests invited to the same party standing on the doorstep before they have been introduced.

That night the members of the wedding, Caroline with Eva Braun's blonde hair, a contingent of Dimonts and a hundred identical twenty-five-year-olds swarmed into the Loudoun Road house, overflowing the sitting room and gloomy dining room, settling where they could, on the stairs, the landings, in the kitchen. John suggested that he and Penny should rent my basement; I said I didn't think it suitable for a baby. Charles rambled on with reminiscences of The Butts and the anthroposophists. Humphrey protested that I should sweep down a marble staircase as mother of them all. Paul, reunited with Humphrey, astonishingly wept. Clive looked sprightly about, Jocelyn was enigmatic. Jeremy propped up the wall and talked to his half-sisters' half-sister, young Sarah Dimont. Sally listened gravely to the drunken ramblings of Charles and Humphrey, neither of whom she knew. Chloe and various dogs barked. I hurried between two ex-husbands, one ex-lover, the daughter and nephews of Deborah's illegitimate father, their wives and husbands, Deborah's illegitimate uncle and cousins and felt — what? Perhaps what one is said to feel when drowning, but I have never drowned, so I don't know. I was gleaning for *Agatha*, and remember thinking 'When I write it, the fact that the founder of the whole thing is alone with Chloe must appear as an advantage, a liberation.'

When I came downstairs in the morning there were messages of 'Thank You' all over the house and someone had written 'We Love You' on the mucky rear window of my car.

5

Back at the cottage in the warmth and silence, white mist outside, I was almost at home. Deb's wedding seemed to have brought *Agatha* nearer. I had an urgent feeling that if I kept digging and sifting I should find she was all there.

No, she isn't. In the last eight years triviality has set in. What happened? I got water-logged, grief-logged. The way out of that must be in understanding. I want nothing but to stay here alone, the perilous dive into it all, the tunnelling.

I am valuable and I will write that value down. Everything else can wait.

CHAPTER
NINETEEN

1

I sat in my room at Yaddo, window open but securely
meshed against mosquitoes and listened to the sound of
somebody else's typewriter, insistent as a cricket. I stared
out at the parched lawn, the jagged shade of surrounding
pines. The temperature was in the nineties. I had been
sitting there for twenty-one days. Thirty-five to go, and
I'd written nothing. *Agatha* seemed beyond me. My
publishers expected *Eighth Street*, and that was what I
was trying to do.

I've known torments of various sorts but none of
them compares with the agony of not being able to write.
What am I trying to say? Search desperately through an
accumulated jumble of words. This one? Those two? In
what order? This way round or that? Misfits, bits of old
sentences. Switch them about long enough and they may
make a cliché. Read it over and over again. Move it
about, dismember it, put it in italics, in quotes, puncture
it with semi-colons, read it. It's still a cliché. Throw it
out, start again. *What am I trying to say?* The sky is
blue. The man is tall. The woman is fat. He said, she
whispered, he shouted, she laughed, he mumbled, she

protested, he declared, she stated. I have nothing to say.

At Yaddo, writer's block was commonplace, symptoms discussed, remedies eagerly offered. I was too proud to admit to mine, but it must have been clear from my hang-dog expression and general air of exhaustion. Distraction was what I needed. George Balanchine was taking a class at the Saratoga Arts Center, why didn't I go? Why not? A few more hours wasted wouldn't make any difference.

We sat on the floor, propping ourselves against the mirrored wall. Invertebrate dancers in ragged leg-warmers and threadbare vests, arms like floating fronds, never shifting their gaze from their mimicking reflections, spun, ran, leapt, to old pop tunes pounded out by an elderly woman on an upright piano. Balanchine, sloppy in sandals, snapped his fingers, sometimes their necks. There was a strong smell of sweat, floor polish, cigarette smoke.

I don't know what happened to me during those few hours. I certainly didn't have a revelation but something broke, shifted, almost as though there had been an hormonal change. I went back to my room, pulled the paper out of the typewriter, threw it away and began *Long Distance.*

Could it really have been so easy? It seemed to be. All the vague, inchoate masses of *Agatha* focused into one clear image: the room I was seeing at that moment, the woman who, at that moment, I actually was. This real place, with its people, relationships, anxieties, could expand to contain the past, even the future. The story would unravel minute by minute, each character and incident bringing with it the shadow of its own history. All I had to do was observe and report what happened.

I addressed the narrative to 'you', either singular or plural, and wrote in the historic present — a tense I dislike, but there seemed no alternative. Begin at the beginning. I am arriving at Yaddo. 'Mrs April opens the door (a side door, one can always recognise them) in the same moment that she says "I am Mrs April."' I climb the stairs, noting every detail — the portraits, the great stained glass window, the fountain, the landing, the lamps. I enter my room — this room. I was careful to be exact. The room measured twenty-seven of my feet by twenty-two, had three doors and contained two beds, one rocking chair, and no less than four dressing tables.

Within the security of this framework I could fly, soar, plunge, play with my life in any way I chose. Every relationship, sight and sound I experienced during those thirty-five days was faithfully recorded and became a springboard into an equally real world of association and memory. I knew Basil Gondzik, I fell in love with Simon; I actually did go to the Fair, swim in the pool, watch an entertainment on the lawn, walk through the woods, stand by the lake. Simultaneously my father grabbed me among my grandmother's vegetables, my mother poked her stick through pine needles in shadow. After weeping at the entertainment, showing myself vulnerable, I was taken to Harben Road, somewhere in the woods, and given the Herculean task of ordering chaos. On my release I tried to escape from this place, Yaddo, my life, but my father was treacherous and took me back. They sent me to Greenways, the West Wing, to teach me how to conform. I was allowed only one visitor, Simon, whom they thought harmless. He was twenty-four, small as a lankly long-haired child. After our short, remarkable love affair he left Yaddo, went away. The Establishment invited me to join it, promising all its benefits if only I would behave suitably to my age and abilities. I began the slow process of dividing into the two selves I had sensed as a child when I wrote the poem about lacquered fingers, worried about in the Caprice with Michael Joseph, finally recognised in the Algonquin Hotel a year before. One self took the Establishment's bribes and tapped off in high heels to its offices somewhere behind the Yaddo garage. The other (myself?) stayed in the rocking chair, drawing maps and thinking of children.

Long Distance was, to me, the most important achievement of my career. This inadequate summary gives little indication of the pleasure it gave me to set facts tumbling around in time, to reach for Oedipus, Peter Pan, Jesus, Hiawatha and drop them into place in the framework of Yaddo 1973. I used fable without respect, reality without conscience. Neither respect nor conscience were relevant to what I was trying to describe.

2

The last time I saw my mother I took as a farewell present an admiring piece about her I had written for some forgotten magazine. She read it with an expression of growing disbelief, then slammed the magazine down.

'What rubbish! How *can* you write such rubbish?'

I mumbled that it was all true.

'But why in the world should anybody want to *read* such a thing?'

The rejection was intolerable. I flared up. 'Maybe because I wrote it!'

She flushed and gave a little sniff. Her back stiffened, her mouth pinched. Still too big for your boots, I see. We parted uncomfortably, in anger.

There was a message for me on the table at Yaddo saying I should ring Con Ed for a cable. I knew my mother had been taken to hospital, but didn't feel particularly worried. It was insufferably hot in the 'phone box and I propped the door open with my foot as I waited. The walls were scrawled with names and 'phone numbers. The operator said, 'Gran died this morning will ring tonight great love Carrie. You want a copy?'

I don't remember running so fast, with such effort, except in dreams. Out of the back door, down the drive, along a track: a huddle of studios, brawny Natalie chiselling stone. I flung myself at her, wailing, babbling. She rocked me, then washed the snot out of my hair and took me back to my room. There were notes (as in Positano, notes were the lifeblood of Yaddo) and somebody left a bottle of wine. Simon crept in as though to a sickroom, talked a little in a hushed voice and crept out again.

This brief outburst seemed the extent of my mourning. The next day I went on working as usual. Chapter 21. My mother, the old woman, was pottering round my grandmother's vegetable garden.

'I'm so glad to see you. They told me you were dead.'

I can see now that the whole of this period was classically manic, pride before the inevitable fall. All I knew then was that I was vibrating, tense, in a kind of sensual ecstasy. It wasn't comfortable, but I relished it more than comfort. After *Long Distance* was finished I spent a few days in New York while Rachel Mackenzie read the manuscript. *The New Yorker* decided to publish the entire book, the first time they had done such a thing since Salinger's *Raise High The Roofbeam Carpenter*. Exulting, I pranced on air over to the East Side to be photographed in the wind by Jill Krementz and we went on to visit Kurt Vonnegut in his apartment on East 54th Street. I saw a long, low room, glass doors opening on a yard flanked on two sides by sheer cliffs. I was rich, and said, 'I want it', not knowing why or for what purpose. Vonnegut said, 'You can have it. We're moving.'

I returned to Loudoun Road to be welcomed by my three elder daughters, beautiful, good, efficient middle-class girls talking about babies, dogs, property. I was light miles away, too remote to recognise that they were mourning their grandmother. At the same time they were so close I could feel the texture of their hair, see the smallest blemish on their smooth skin, hear their furtive muttering:

'Mum's been liberated.'

'Bloody good thing if you ask me.'

To prove it I took Caroline and Julia to the Caribbean.

3

I find it hard now to imagine anything more doomed than a manic fifty-five-year-old woman and her two nervous grown-up daughters isolated in a package hotel at the end of an airstrip in St Lucia. Grey heat, 'cottages' with corrugated iron roofs, a few yards of beach swarming with mosquitoes and old cans, a swimming pool prettily situated in the car park, pink British in Caribbean shirts and woollen socks, the endless din of electric guitars and maracas. This, anyway, is how I saw it about a week after our arrival. I had been bursting with joy and the two normal young women seemed to me stern, authoritarian, middle-aged. I was prone to paranoia at the best of times; now I began to imagine they not only disapproved, but disliked me, could barely survive my company.

A considerable laugher in my way, I haven't laughed for days. Not even giggled. Stuck here in the pouring rain with Goneril and Regan and inedible food. Is there anywhere on St Lucia I could buy Lear? A joke not to be shared, and not very durable.

'I think I'll just nip into Castries.'
'What on earth for?'
'Well . . . see if I can get Shakespeare.'
'Mother, you're *mad*!' They were calling me 'Mother' at that time, rather than 'Mum'.

After a long search round Castries I tracked down the Collected Works in what may have been a school basement. For the rest of the day I lay on my stretcher and read: ' . . . ever since thou madest thy daughters thy mother; . . .when thou gavest them the rod, and puttest down thine own breeches . . .' . By the evening I had acquired a novel. I've grown familiar with it over the years and nourish it constantly. It will probably stay with me for the rest of my life.

Lear loved Goneril no doubt, and no doubt Goneril wasn't the pantomime monster she appears; but connived with Regan to make a place for herself, to become the dead or absent mother. Back in Loudoun Road I was haunted, as I had never been during my mother's lifetime. I stopped writing (she had never approved of it) and spent my days obsessively cleaning the house to no purpose.

Kurt wrote that I was missing the crocuses, the flowering crab would be out in six weeks. The vague image of a hideout, a hole in the ground that could be covered with bracken, somewhere even my children could never find, alternated with the even vaguer image of successful novelist, soignée at dinner parties. Determined to survive until the apartment was empty, I started jumping from one stepping-stone to the next, always taking my lifelong luggage in case I should never return.

This period, like many others, is remembered as a series of dreams: Derek Hart took me to a party where the hostess delivered a lantern lecture on cunts, identifying each slide by its astrological sign: 'This one is Libra, she is six foot tall', 'This one is Scorpio, she's a prostitute who had her labia stripped and her clitoris sheathed.' Dejected guests in frayed denim lounging round a huge hot swimming pool, Jonathan Miller like a great tapir, Dee Wells not speaking to Professor Ayer, who spoke mostly to the girl showing the lantern slides; Antonia Fraser, exquisite as usual, sitting the entire evening on a small sofa, her expression placid, as though about to moo.

Belgravia: balancing baked potatoes with sour cream

and great ladles of caviar on our sixteen middle-aged knees before going downstairs for a silver dish of rare sirloin, eaten off silver plates; George Axelrod protesting that everything was 'dumb' – God, politics, life in general: just dumb; Kenneth Tynan managing to introduce at least two 'fucks' into every sentence, then, still hopeful, trying to badger us into playing risqué parlour games; his wife Kathy accepting ten pounds from Axelrod for some won wager; Tynan muttering, the exchange of money making a sudden icy awkwardness. *If they found me dull and badly dressed I don't care – dying on their Gucci feet to the tick tock of their Cartier watches.*

I had a sticker on my car, brought from New York: IMPEACH THE COX-SACKER it said. I went to stay with Paul and Jay in their thatched 'cottage' in Oxfordshire: My brother read the sticker with a pinched expression. Please would I reverse my car into the drive instead of parking it nose forward? The village might not understand . . . *Disapproval. No jokes. Plod plod. Jesus.*

Stephen Spender grumbling that someone had been 'raving about some trash.' 'My book,' I said, then had to work hard to get him back to a better humour. Calling on old Madam Gimpels, sitting in the back room of the gallery in Davies Street. Roland Penrose was there. 'Roland and Stephen think they're important,' she said, 'but my dear, you're much more important.' Horrified by such blasphemy, I giggled. She wept a little about her husband being dead and what an effect my writing had on people. 'There is no way out of isolation,' she said. I kissed her cheek; she made me kiss the other and promise to visit her again. I never did.

Giving a reading from *Long Distance* in a converted

garage, now an art gallery. Paintings by Stephen Buckley hung despondently on the walls. Apart from a quick glance at Jeremy, I didn't look at the audience. When it was over there was dead silence, like church. My agent's tears, she said, washed out her contact lenses.

Kurt cabled that they had moved out, the apartment was mine. When I went to say goodbye to Barry Cooper he took a grave view of my condition and gave me a prescription for Ritalin and three different kinds of uppers. I flew to New York, spent a few days with Vonnegut and Jill Krementz in their elegant brownstone and finally, on 20th April 1974, moved in to 349 East 54th Street.

5

The apartment was bare, not a mug or teaspoon. Chattering to myself like a bird in a bush I hammered, painted, lugged home bits of scrap, assembled do-it-yourself furniture from inscrutable diagrams, flew in and out of Bloomingdales, accumulated possessions. Cab drivers asked for dates, the owner of the junk shop promised to take care of me, Bloomingdales' delivery man said he would find me a rich boyfriend, flowers and fruit and asparagus spilled from doorways of front-room shops, towers of black ice glittered, the river flicked up its oily surface in the Spring sunshine. *Long Distance* was in *The New Yorker*. I was happy. My mother kept quiet until it was finished, nothing more to do; then, as I was admiring it, she tracked me down: 'Very nice, dear, but rather pointless, don't you think? What are you going to do now?' I had no idea — live in it, I suppose.

All my so-called independent places – the Studio, the flats in Ascona and Aberdare Gardens, the house in Loudoun Road - had been crowded with John and the children. 349 East 54th Street was virgin territory. I knew a few people - Tony Godwin, recently moved to New York, Penelope Gilliatt, Howard Moss, Edmund White from Yaddo, a young film-cutter called Lawrence, helpful at mending and fixing, who read passages of Ovid to the tape recorder to test it and stood on his head for long periods. Jill Krementz told me that what she heard about *Long Distance* made her wonder if they were harbouring a weirdo. The Vonnegut guests owned houses in Cape Cod and said things like 'We have a little civil disobedience thing going', there were many aggressive, unattached young women, a few black revolutionaries with their pallid girls, Kurt lounged about, inaccessible, an Oklahoma mechanic looking like a profound thinker. They brought a novelist to dinner, ('he's single' Jill said meaningfully), a man who said 'effing' instead of 'fucking' and got drunk without grace.

Though awkward in Kurt's company, I was fond of him and could even understand some of his laconic remarks. Perhaps he would understand mine. Here I was, I told him, with a book in *The New Yorker* and an apartment, but lonely (a word I always avoided and probably didn't use). He patted my hand and said that his therapist, Dr Martha Friedman, could probably come up with something. Martha was plump, middle-aged, ribald. She wore blouses dizzy with paroquets, dacron slacks, hoop ear rings, a quantity of beads. She told me I was grieving for my mother. Seeing she's dead, I said, that's probably true. Martha granted me this, so I began to talk. After listening for some time – nodding vehemently, expostulating, roaring with laughter — she picked up the 'phone and dialled a number, her expression that of a poker player about to produce a straight flush.

'I've got Penelope Mortimer here. You need her in Human Relations.'

There was an excited cackle on the other end. '... There you are, then ... Thursday morning. OK, I'll tell her ... *Long Distance* changed her life,' Martha remarked wryly as she put the 'phone down, 'Or so she says.'

That was how I came to be offered the unlikely job of teaching Creative Writing at The New School for Social Research on West 12th Street. I knew nothing about teaching and only had the haziest idea what 'Creative Writing' meant, but a choice of some sort had been made. From September on I would live permanently in New York. Meanwhile I returned to England to sort out and try to dispose of the past.

6

When I got back to London, pre-publication copies of *Long Distance* had already been sent out. Harold rang to say he thought it a major work, comparable only with Becket ('I kiss your hand, I kiss your mouth, I kiss your feet'); Jonathan Miller pronounced it 'extraordinary' and told me I was like Isaac Newton, whose life apparently changed dramatically in middle age; Ronnie Harwood sent a succinct postcard: 'It's a masterpiece.' These were connoisseurs' reactions and I was still doubtful.

At the tame little launch party those journalists who could read mumbled 'hard going'. Again all the newspapers were on strike on publication day. When the notices began coming in the posh papers found the book enthralling, impressive, mysterious but precise, limpid but unfathomable, an experiment which suggested interesting possibilities for The Novel, a work of conscious literary insight and wit; the rest damned it as obscure, nutty as a fruit cake, an indulgence, a mishandling of fantasy. Auberon Waugh was so outraged that he forgot the past three years of decimal currency: '... Psychiatrists expect to be paid twelve guineas an hour for pretending to listen to this sort of ego-maniac drivel.'

It hadn't occurred to any of them that the location could be a real place, or that the book was an embellished report of events that had actually happened during a specific time. Why should it? None of them had been there; none of them knew me, except through my previous work. I was irritated by the hostility, grateful for the praise, but not particularly impressed by either. The writer they were praising or deriding wasn't me; the book they were talking about wasn't the book I had written. *Long Distance* crept on to the bestseller list with Solzhenitsyn and Len Deighton, slid rapidly off and disappeared.

Stable Cottage was put on the market. I occupied myself by clearing out drawer after drawer of unused or broken machinery, twenty-five-year-old toys, rags of 'dressing up' clothes, torn snapshots, long lost socks. The movers came and took away the furniture. The place was emptied of everything except twelve, sixteen, seventeen-year-old Jeremy, a few drawing pins and an indelible smell of frying. It had been the nearest approach to home since Harben Road, but I left it with curiously little regret.

CHAPTER TWENTY

1

I taught at the New School in New York from September 1974 until June 1975. That September I moved to Boston University as 'visiting professor' and stayed there until May 1977. In retrospect it is almost as though I was anaesthetised during those years, coming round only on the frequent occasions I flew or sailed back to England.

You can't dip in and out of people's lives and expect to feel part of them. Either stay or go. If both those alternatives are impossible, as they were for me, the only hope is to lower your expectations of both and be grateful for the meagre results. I hadn't the sense or the ability to do this, and gradually became displaced, drifting in limbo between a past I mourned and a future I began to fear. A quotation from Nathaniel Hawthorne's *The Marble Faun* was pinned to the wall in front of my desk:

The years, after all, have a kind of emptiness when we spend too many of them on a foreign shore. We defer the reality of life ... until a future moment, when we shall again breathe our native air; but by and by there are no future moments; or, if we do return, we find that the native air has lost its invigorating quality. Thus, between two countries, we have none at all, or only that little space of either in which we finally lay down our discontented bones. It is wise, therefore, to come back betimes, or never.

Much later I framed it, along with a snapshot of myself holding Jeremy's son.

2

Many things had happened while I was away: Caroline had left Leslie Phillips and was living alone with her dogs, Deborah's second son was a year old, Jeremy finishing his third year at Oxford, David Mercer married and sober; Madelon and Lee were back in London and the house in Loudoun Road had been sold. With my half of the proceeds I bought what seemed to be a suitable flat almost within sight of John Barnes; that it was in the same road as Caroline's was, I persuaded myself, a happy coincidence. My bedroom was a basement, but the living room had french windows opening onto a garden and beyond that was a remarkable field — scattered with litter, treeless, but still a field — in which someone kept a scabby old pony. The garden was communal, though seldom used by anyone except my neighbour, a resentful young woman we called 'Powerful Pat'. On hot Sundays she would sit sternly in the middle of it playing her transistor.

I know my daughters hoped I might find a husband in America, but the years of addiction had made that unlikely, if not impossible. Even now I was by no means cured, though the symptoms were disguised under a thin layer of what I called reason. Whatever the pain and fury connected with John as a husband, as an individual he was my only familiar. I hoped we might be friends. If not, there was no reason why our lives should overlap and I must ignore him. But there were far too many undercurrents for friendship and John had become a public figure, impossible to ignore. He beamed out of newspapers, chortled over our 'blood-stained but not boring' marriage, identifying his wives as 'Penny One' and 'Penny Two'. Terry Wogan introduced him as 'the famous lawyer, playwright and womaniser' and simpered at his stories of getting married when he was 'about fourteen' to 'someone with five children'. 'I can't feel loyalty to a wife simply because she's my wife,' John said, smiling benevolently out of my television screen. 'One's only duty and obligation is to oneself.' *A billion solitary egos bumping into each other and not even saying 'sorry'!*, but I couldn't answer back. I protected myself by avoiding anyone who might tell me they had recently met or were about to meet him; virtually everyone, in fact, I had known in the past.

My notebooks contained excellent advice: *Get a job. Don't beg, don't rush. Observe other people's lives. WORK.* I had enjoyed teaching and knew I was good at it, however eccentric my methods. There was a scribbled letter from Boston saying I made 'an enormous difference' to my students and was 'a vivid, bright, smart and compassionate presence', but even translated into English this didn't sound much of a qualification. I wrote to Manchester Polytechnic – presumably they advertised for a writer in residence or something of the sort – but there was no reply. Someone suggested the Royal College of Art might be interested, so I contacted Christopher Cornford and he wasn't. I lunched with Karl Miller in Heal's restaurant, crammed at a table with three women and their carrier bags. He said he was sure I'd have no difficulty finding something, so we talked about Robert Frost. I was interviewed for a job at the City Literary Institute but didn't get it. Clearly I was never going to make my living in England by teaching.

As a writer, however, there was a good chance of survival; even of success, if that had been what I wanted. *Encounter* printed an otherwise unsaleable short story; *The Times* bought a chapter of *About Time* for its Christmas Eve issue; Peter Crookston, then editor of the *Observer Colour Magazine*, offered me a retainer for six articles a year and generously let me go my own way after realising that it was no good asking me to cover race riots in Stockholm. I went to Cornwall and interviewed W. S. Graham:

'Tell my about your parents.'

'My dear. You must ask me something very small. Like "Why do you put capitals at the beginning of the lines of your verse?"'

'Why do you put capitals at the beginning of the lines of your verse?'

'To make people realise it's poetry.'

'Tell me about you parents.'

'My dear. I thought you had come here to find out my relationship to my own poetry or verse. Do you not want to know what I think about my own poetry?'

'Yes I do. But it would be impertinent of me to try and write anything about your poetry.'

'My dear. I already love you and you can say anything. Ask me and I will answer.'

'Tell me about your parents.'

'I thought I was going to speak to you for a wee while, although this is lovely and I'd rather speak to you all the time, all your life if you like. But the number of words

you're going to get into this is very small. After all this talk I think you could write a novel. Go away, I'll write the bugger myself!'

I never did learn about Graham's parents. He asked if I would drive him round for a wee while. We stopped at the pub for a half-bottle of whisky and drove to the Lanyon Quoit. A lark hovered, twittering and fussing: the first one, he told me. Finally I wrote down a list of questions and wedged them under his back door. Two days later, when I was leaving, he gave me an envelope which, he said contained his answers;

> *Make, for your work's sake, the best thing*
> *So that it's great entertainment to read.*
> *At least the lark decided to show off*
> *And soar and sing above us singing Penelope*
> *What are you getting out of Sydney.*

After that I interviewed Canon Wilfred Wood of Catford and we recited 'Lord, support us all the day long of this troublous life until the shadows lengthen and the evening comes . . .' in unison as we drove back from a funeral, laughing with pleasure at the words. Wilfred Wood made me realise that there actually were good people in the world, men of some sort of God. Years later, when idly wondering who would conduct my funeral, I looked him up in Crockford's. Discovering that he had become Bishop of Croydon, I decided it was unlikely he would be able to spare the time.

Lear's daughters still muttered in a corner, but after what I felt to be the rejection of *Long Distance* I was fearful of another novel. Hired to write the script of *Death of a Princess*, I spent three weeks with the director,

Anthony Thomas, in Beirut and Saudi Arabia. Six months later I resigned, just as I had resigned from *Tarnowska* and *Charles Dilke*. In the halcyon days before the success of *Pumpkin Eater* writing had been associated with joy, an obsessed excitement much like being in love. When it came to expressing other people's ideas, writing to a formula, my only skill locked itself in a kind of *vaginismus*.

If this were a novel my protagonist would now review her journey through the past sixty years in lucid and probably poetic prose, realising that she had reached a major cross-roads. Her problem would be clear, her confusion (through my understanding of it) articulate. Then would come a resolution of some sort. To return to the original metaphor, she could discipline her father's daughter, despatch Ginger into suitable retirement and choose her mother's child as the most reliable persona in which to approach old age and death. On the other hand she could go off at a tangent, take up politics or God, emigrate, commit murder. The possibilities would be endless.

Writing an autobiography also entails inventing a simplified, recognisable character. Selection and capricious memory remove the story further from absolute truth, but from then on the most one can do is to hold a mirror to the past and try to describe its reflection. At this point of my story all I can see is a room in West Hampstead, the bed I bought in Bloomingdales, the desk I carted home in a box from Second Avenue, a table bought for my apartment in Cambridge, a wall of books accumulated in Harben Road, Aberdare Gardens, Holland Park, Stable Cottage. There is an illegible notebook and a typewriter on the desk, photographs, a dirty coffee cup and saucer, the ashtrays have been used. But if I exist in this room, which is by no means certain, I am invisible. In other words I don't know who I was and the clues remain meaningless. Layer upon layer of images – daughter, woman, wife, mother, writer, lover, teacher – had formed an impenetrable crust over whoever I was in the first place. The outside world identified me as 'ex-wife of John Mortimer, mother of six, author of *The Pumpkin Eater*' –accurate, as far as it went, but to me unrecognisable.

In hindsight I can see that this period may have been like despair before a novel, a time of gestation, and that something – a memory, the sensation of a memory – must have been stirring. 'It's always darkest before dawn,' my mother might have said, if she too hadn't disappeared. In any case I have no rational explanation for what followed.

I was slowly and thoroughly reading the *Sunday Times* and had got as far as the Property Column:

COTSWOLDS. Listed stone cottage in unspoiled village. Open plan living-kitchen area, open fireplace, mullions, 2 bedrooms, big attic, study with picture window, bathroom, C.H. 1 acre garden with exceptional views Manor House & Evenlode valley. Ideal retreat for writer or artist. £26,000 o.n.o. Tel. 01 387 2077 or Barton-on-the-Heath.

It was something to do. I rang the London number – no reply. Presumably the owners were weekending in numberless Barton on the Heath. The vague whim took on an extraordinary urgency and over the next few days I tried again and again, still without success. Finally I rang the *Sunday Times*. Sorry, they said, must have been a typo.

The following day I drove to the Cotswolds and bought the cottage and its acre within half-an-hour of walking up the front path.

CHAPTER
TWENTY-ONE

1

Chastleton is a backwater hamlet, notable only for its Jacobean manor house. In 1978 the oldest inhabitant, Harry Newnam, lived in the one cottage still belonging to the estate; its thatch was sagging, there was no water or electricity, but Harry had planted the rose *La France* by the front door and his bedding plants were a rare sight. At one time, he told me, all the village women would collect on the bank outside my cottage to gossip on summer evenings. He showed me mottled brown photographs of Edward VII and Queen Alexandra driving in a barouche through the gateway of The House at the start of a country weekend. Women with eighteen-inch waists and toppling hair would have sauntered with their beaux round the topiary, the sound of violins and confident sopranos could have been heard from my garden.

Now, no longer dependent on the House, the village had an orphaned quality, like a country divorced from its city. A ravishingly beautiful dovecote was stranded in the vestiges of parkland, the Norman church, once a domestic chapel, was damp and dilapidated, used once a month by a commuting parson and the families of two or three gentlemen farmers; the House itself, said to be the only unrestored Jacobean building in the country, suffered from years of neglect, its garden a wilderness of brambles, the yew chopped by a local farmer into shapes vaguely resembling Mickey Mouse and Donald Duck. Only the monumental trees wore their age with dignity. They towered over the lane, their ancient arms creaking in the wind, refuge for ten thousand generations of birds.

The Old Post Office was one of a pair of semi-detached cottages, square, plain and unassuming, built in 1708 for the Manor's coachman and head gardener. The only relic of its short career as a village Post Office was a pillar box with a bas-relief of George V's profile set in the gatepost. The ceilings were low, even to me, and heavily beamed, the steep staircase so narrow that generations of corpses had to be humped down and coffined in the kitchen. An ugly little concrete box had been added to serve as a bathroom and the previous owner had built a lean-to study, otherwise it remained unchanged since the ground floor was tiled sometime in the 19th century. The garden, which originally consisted of a strip in front − sweet alyssum, I'm sure, soapwort, clary, canterbury bells − and a long strip at the back for cabbages, pigsty and privy, had been extended over the years and was now a substantial area, the cause of much envy and hostility from the neighbours .

I sold the flat and dug myself in. Owning land made some stubbornly preserved part of me emerge rampant, sweeping the rest out of sight. Land didn't just mean the surface, a measurable extent of grass and soil, buildings and trees. It meant subsoil, clay, shale, grit, limestone, rock, worms, larvae, unimaginable life down to the centre of the earth where, I imagined, it changed ownership and became the ocean floor, a desert island, possibly the proud property of some Antipodean bungalow. A childish idea, but I rapidly reverted to childhood, with the added advantage of appearing elderly and responsible.

Jim Clark, one of my Boston students, hitched most of the way from Oregon and turned up with his backpack and typewriter. He slept on the floor in the bare attic and industriously tapped at his writing most of the day; in the evenings he would settle like a tangible vapour by the fire or sit for hours in the field, presumably meditating. After he left I expected loneliness. Days, weeks went by; I waited, but it didn't come. The profound relief of escaping from what I thought of as John's world, of knowing the family was far away but would sometimes visit, gave me a sense of safety I had never experienced, or couldn't remember experiencing before. At night there was no sound but creaking timbers and the wind. I tucked my feet up from the draught, coughed in the wood-smoke, never tired of looking: all mine — ancient beams, thick walls, worm-eaten floorboards, chimney, moss on the roof, wind, garden. The future cleared, spread out in seasons. For the first time in my life - anyway the first time I could remember — I could savour the present, the pleasure of being alive at this moment. The past surfaced only in dreams, most curiously filled with love.

Index